Twelve military heroes.
Twelve indomitable heroines.
One UNIFORMLY HOT! miniseries.

Don't miss a story in Harlequin Blaze's
12-book continuity series, featuring irresistible
soldiers from all branches of the armed forces.

Now serving—
those reckless and wild flyboys in the U.S. Air Force...

TAILSPIN
by Cara Summers
July 2011

HOT SHOT
by Jo Leigh
August 2011

NIGHT MANEUVERS
by Jillian Burns
September 2011

Uniformly Hot!—
The Few. The Proud. The Sexy as Hell!

Dear Reader,

I thoroughly enjoyed writing *Tailspin,* my second contribution to Harlequin Blaze's Uniformly Hot! miniseries. There's something irresistible about a man in uniform… And my Air Force fighter pilot, Captain Nash Fortune, is a prime example....

When Nash Fortune was nineteen and a cadet at the air force academy, he fell in love with seventeen-year-old Bianca Quinn. It was the kind of reckless love that defies reason. But she backed out of their plans to elope. Worse, she accepted a bribe from his grandmother to disappear from his life.

Eleven years have passed, and Bianca—now a successful writer—is back in Nash's life and asking for his help on a story that involves a missing cadet, a former classmate of his. The problem is that he wants her just as intensely as he always did. Once again, she's sending him into a tailspin, and it will take all of his skills to pull out of it safely. That is, if he wants to....

I believe in second chances. They're always riskier than the first ones. I hope you'll enjoy Bianca's and Nash's story as much as I enjoyed writing it, and that you'll look for Nash's friend Jonah's story in December.

Happy endings always!

Cara Summers

Cara Summers

TAILSPIN

Harlequin®

TORONTO NEW YORK LONDON
AMSTERDAM PARIS SYDNEY HAMBURG
STOCKHOLM ATHENS TOKYO MILAN MADRID
PRAGUE WARSAW BUDAPEST AUCKLAND

Recycling programs
for this product may
not exist in your area.

ISBN-13: 978-0-373-79626-7

TAILSPIN

ABOUT THE AUTHOR

Was Cara Summers born with the dream of becoming a published romance novelist? No. But now that she is, she still feels her dream has come true. She loves writing for the Harlequin Blaze line because it allows her to create strong, determined women and seriously sexy men who will risk everything to achieve their dreams. Cara has written more than thirty-five novels for Harlequin Books, and when she isn't working on new stories, she teaches in the writing program at Syracuse University and at a community college near her home.

Books by Cara Summers

To get the inside scoop on Harlequin Blaze and its talented writers, be sure to check out blazeauthors.com.

Don't miss any of our special offers. Write to us at the following address for information on our newest releases.

Harlequin Reader Service
U.S.: 3010 Walden Ave., P.O. Box 1325, Buffalo, NY 14269
Canadian: P.O. Box 609, Fort Erie, Ont. L2A 5X3

To Lt. Col. Ray "Borg" Bowen,
Commander and Professor of Aerospace Studies
at Syracuse University. Thank you so much for the
time you spent explaining to me what it means
to be in the Air Force and to fly fighter planes.
My story is so much richer because of you, and
I will treasure being an honorary "Airman" forever.

Prologue

PERFECT TIMING, Maggie Fortune thought as she climbed out of her red Corvette. The nearly empty parking lot told her that the noon Mass at the Church of St. Francis had ended so she and Father Mike Flynn could meet right away.

That suited her fine. What didn't suit her was that even the fast ride in her sporty convertible hadn't quite settled her nerves. Her birthday party started at five, but thanks to her houseman Grady, all the details had been seen to. It was her meeting with Father Mike that was making her nervous.

Ridiculous. She hurried toward the church. She'd known the priest when she'd been plain old Maggie Nash. They'd gone to grade school together. He'd married her to her late husband, Thaddeus Fortune IV, and he'd held her hand at the funerals of her husband and of her sons. And it wasn't that she was up to anything that was morally wrong. She just wanted to cover all her bases.

So why were her hands damp? Damn it! Damn them!

She started up the long flight of stairs that led to the

front door, taking pride in the fact that although she was celebrating her seventy-fifth birthday, she wasn't short of breath when she reached the top.

Well, not very short of breath. Still, she caught herself taking a few deep ones as she hurried up the center aisle of the church. Dim light filtered through stained glass, but she made out a few people still lingering on the side altar where the statue of St. Francis stood enclosed in a glass case.

As her eyes grew more accustomed to the dimness, she watched the small group turn away and descend the steps. Then she spotted Father Mike still standing in front of the statue. Perfect, she thought again. She'd be in and out of here in fifteen minutes. Tops.

Her talent for timing things well had been helpful throughout her life and especially since her husband's death twenty years ago when she'd taken over the job of running the Fortune family's various business interests. In the corporate world, timing could be everything. And it was equally important in personal matters, too.

As she drew closer, Father Mike dropped to his knees to say a prayer. Not wanting to intrude, Maggie halted and let her gaze lift to the statue. It looked as small and unassuming as the first time she'd seen it. Originally, the marble figure had been donated to the Franciscan Capuchin order by an Italian family who'd immigrated to Denver from Assisi, Italy, where the saint had been born. Since that time, the statue of St. Francis had gained an ever increasing reputation for granting petitioners' prayers. Nothing on the scale of a major miracle or anything like that. But people believed that the statue had some kind of special pull with God.

Back in February, the *Denver Post* had run an article containing story after story of how a visit to the statue had resulted in prayers being answered and lives being changed. The narratives ran the gamut of lovers being united, babies being conceived to families meeting up with lost loved ones.

Still studying the figure of St. Francis, she let her mind drift back fifteen years to the first time she'd encountered the statue. It had stood in the small garden next to the St. Francis Center for Boys. Father Mike had run afternoon and weekend programs there, and she still credited him with keeping her grandson Nash out of jail. Of course, Father Mike had always passed on any credit to St. Francis.

True, the prayers she'd said to the statue that first time in the prayer garden might have played a role. But Maggie was certain that if Nash hadn't been able to occupy his after school and weekend hours at the center, and if it hadn't been for the friends he'd made there, well…she doubted he'd be a captain in the Air Force today. And that had been his goal ever since he'd lost his father in the Gulf War.

That had been a terrible time for them both. Within a year, she'd lost a husband and a son. She'd had to take over the running of Fortune Enterprises and at the same time raise a seven-year-old boy who was a magnet for trouble.

Not that Nash was ever a bad boy. But he was impatient, impulsive and pretty damn creative when it came to getting into mischief. Qualities he'd probably inherited from her.

When his pranks had gotten him kicked out of two private schools in a year, she'd become desperate. And guilt ridden. She owed Father Mike big time. And the center. Okay, perhaps she owed St. Francis, too.

The priest rose and turned to face her just as she

stepped to the foot of the altar. He hadn't changed much at all in the time she'd known him. The eyes with their kindness and twinkle of mischief were still the same. Okay, the hair was definitely whiter, but his smile was just as brilliant as ever. And the aura of holiness was there as it always had been.

"Maggie, you look amazing."

"I was just thinking the same about you." When he held out his arms, she walked right into them and returned his hug. Her tension eased just a little.

Stepping back, he held on to her hands and studied her for a moment. "You said you wanted to talk to me about something. Is it your health?"

"No. I'm fine." She'd had a recent bout of breast cancer, but so far she was on the winning end of that battle.

He gestured her toward the front row of pews and sat beside her. "What brings you to St. Francis?"

"The short answer is the same person who brought me to you and St. Francis eleven years ago."

"Bianca Quinn?"

"Yes. I need your advice."

"You're always welcome to that—for what it's worth."

Maggie flicked a glance toward the statue, then met his eyes again. "Is it possible to reverse a prayer?"

"Reverse?" He asked the question in a musing tone and seemed to think about it for a moment. "Prayers aren't like spells or curses. But you could certainly say a new one and tell St. Francis just what you want."

"You remember what I asked him to help me with eleven years ago."

"I do. You asked me to help you also. And you succeeded in persuading Bianca Quinn not to elope with your grandson, Nash. I was there in the room when she signed the agreement."

Maggie studied him for a moment. She'd asked him to come that day because Bianca had thought so highly of him, and she'd known that his presence would add weight to her argument. But she'd never been sure that he'd entirely approved of what she'd done. She lifted her chin. "I did the right thing. I haven't changed my mind about that. And," she gestured toward the statue, "he answered that prayer better than I could have imagined. He filled in blanks I couldn't have foreseen. Nash not only graduated from the Air Force Academy, he's earned a medal of honor for his courage and is an exceptional pilot. And now Bianca is a published writer. She's at the start of a wonderful career. If they'd gone through with their plans to marry, I doubt they'd be where they are today."

"Then what's troubling you, Maggie?"

She waved a hand. "I didn't think to pray for all of that to happen. I only prayed that I could convince her to go away."

"But you wanted them both to succeed in their careers and to be happy, didn't you?"

"Yes, I suppose." She wasn't aware until Father Mike put his hand over hers that she'd clasped them tightly together in her lap. Why in the world was she still so nervous? She'd gotten through board meetings and negotiated deals without batting an eye. And all she had to deal with here was a saint and a statue that had so far answered all her prayers with regard to her grandson.

"What do you want now, Maggie?"

"I want them to find again the kind of happiness that they found with each other when they were younger. I think they might belong together, the way I belonged with my Thad. He was it for me. I knew it the first time I looked at him. I think it may have been the same for Nash and Bianca."

"Why do you think that?"

"Well, they haven't found anyone else. In spite of the fact that the *Denver Post* chose Nash as one of the area's most eligible bachelors. He's not even bringing a date to my birthday party tonight. And Bianca has been totally focused on building her career."

He smiled at her. "You want St. Francis to bring them back together. There's your prayer. Just say it."

"I don't need to ask for that part. I'm already making sure their paths will cross again. They'll meet again at my birthday party tonight." She jerked her head at the statue. "I'd just like a little backup support. Because this time I want them to have what I took away from them the last time they parted. I want the happily ever after." She paused. Sighed. "But I have a stake in this. It's not just their happiness I want. It's mine, too. I want family. I want Nash to have a family, too. I want grandchildren. I want more Fortune heirs."

With a smile, Father Mike patted her hands. "Just ask St. Francis. The exact words don't matter. He'll know what's in your mind just as he did the last time. Come." He drew her to her feet and up the steps to the altar.

Perhaps it was that simple after all. But she was still tense even after she'd knelt in front of the statue and said her prayer.

Father Mike knelt down beside her. "Now, why don't you ask him for the rest of what you came here for?"

When she turned to stare at him, he continued, "You said the short answer to why you'd come here today was

Bianca Quinn. What's the long answer? You might as well give St. Francis all of it."

Maggie realized that was really what she'd come here to do. So she told Father Mike and St. Francis the rest.

1

SUN BEAT DOWN on the tarmac as Nash Fortune impatiently stopped his small plane just short of the runway. There was still one aircraft ahead of him, and it was filled with both eager and not so eager Air Force Academy cadets who were going up to practice their parachuting skills. The memory of his first jump from a plane had him grinning. That feeling of free-falling through space was the next best thing to flying.

Which was what he was here to do. If the plane ahead of him ever took off.

He figured he had about three hours until he was due at his grandmother's birthday party bash. And each minute that ticked by cut short his flight time.

The morning he'd just put in had made him yearn for some time in the sky. The wind had picked up steadily all day, and more than once he'd found himself looking out of his classroom window. Teaching strategic flight maneuvers in a simulation lab appealed to him on an intellectual level, and it did provide the occasional adrenaline rush. But it wasn't the same as the real thing.

This morning five of his students had asked him to open the lab and give them some extra practice time.

He'd had to talk several young pilots in training into and then out of a tailspin. As he had, he'd known exactly what the kids were feeling—the initial helplessness, followed by the flash of panic. And through it all the excitement of the challenge. Life and death hung on whether or not your reflexes were quick enough, your control strong enough to bring that plane out of a fatal spin. The thrill of meeting that kind of challenge and the ability to handle it was what made him become a pilot.

He'd managed to get all five of his students safely through their simulated maneuvers, but three hours in the lab hadn't relieved the restlessness he'd been experiencing lately. His single-engine Cessna was no fighter jet—far from it. But it was still a little honey of a plane.

His grandmother had given it to him a year ago when he'd started teaching at the Air Force Academy. If she hadn't had health problems, he'd have signed up for a third tour of duty in Afghanistan. She'd argued vehemently against his changing his plans. Her breast cancer was stage one, and a bevy of specialists had assured her that surgery and radiation was the treatment she needed. No chemo. She didn't even have to cut back on her work schedule. She was going to be fine.

But there'd been an opening that suited him in the Department of Military and Strategic Studies at the Air Force Academy, and he was determined to be close at hand when she was going through treatments. He'd lost his mother when he'd been born and his father when he was seven. Maggie Fortune was the only family he had, and vice versa. That meant that when the chips were down, they were a team. After all she'd stuck with him

when he'd gone through that rough patch in his teens.
The least he could do was stick with her now.

He glanced at his watch. Another two minutes had
gone by and the plane in front of him hadn't budged.
In his mind, he pictured the flight instructor running
one last check on the equipment. He bit back a sigh.
Patience had never been his long suit, but he'd had con-
siderably less of it at thirteen. And he'd been so damn
bored. All he could think of was that he had to wait
five more years—eons—until he could apply to the Air
Force Academy. And filling the headmaster's dresser
drawers with frogs had seemed a great way to pass the
time. His classmates would have elected him president
of the student government organization—if he hadn't
been kicked out of the school.

That was when his grandmother had given up on
lecture and logic and sent him to Father Mike Flynn at
the St. Francis Center for Boys.

He'd owe her forever for that decision. Not only had
his boredom been relieved, but he'd made two lifetime
friends, Gabe Wilder and Jonah Stone. Back in those
days, the center and Father Mike had the reputation for
being able to put troubled teens back on track. He supposed that he and his friends could be considered stellar
examples of the program's success. Gabe, the son of
legendary art thief Raphael Wilder, had not turned to a
life of crime. Instead, he now headed up a security firm
that was gaining a nationwide reputation. And Gabe was
getting married soon to an FBI agent who specialized in
white-collar crime. Jonah Stone, a savvy street kid, had
become an equally savvy and successful entrepreneur.
He now owned two nightclubs in San Francisco and a
brand new one in Denver. Both his friends would be at
his grandmother's birthday bash tonight.

So would he. If he ever got off the ground. He sent up a little prayer of thanksgiving as the plane ahead of him finally began to taxi. He waited for it to accelerate, watched it lift, then kept it in sight until it faded to a speck of silver in the brilliant blue sky.

After touching a finger to the medal around his neck, Nash let the Cessna rip. When it lifted, he welcomed the challenge of the windy crosscurrents, relished the bumps as he dipped one wing, leveled off, and nosed upward. The trees on the ridge ahead grew more distinct as they rushed towards him, then blurred as he shot the plane up and over them.

He spared a glance at the land dropping away below, and felt the restlessness begin to disappear. He had an hour to soar, to glide, to simply play in the sky.

His earliest memory of flying was sitting on his dad's lap in the pilot's seat and holding on to the wheel. During the months before his dad had been deployed to the Gulf War, they'd taken several flights together, and he'd graduated to the copilot's seat. His dad had promised to teach him to fly when he returned.

Pushing the memories and the regrets aside, Nash banked the plane, headed east, and climbed again. Today wasn't a day for thinking of anything. It was a day meant for simply flying. When the peaks and valleys below were merely ripples of lighter and darker green, he climbed even higher and took the plane into a first lazy loop.

Laughing, he soared into a second one and a third. Then he decided to execute what his students had been practicing in the lab all day—taking a plane into and out of a spin.

He deliberately made the "mistake" described in all the textbooks, the one he'd coached his students to make in the simulation. He banked the plane to the right, then applied the rudder to suddenly accelerate the rate of the turn. Adrenaline kicked in when he felt the plane stall and saw the nose dip below the horizon. Then the rotation began and the plane went into an uncontrolled spin.

If he hadn't been strapped in, centrifugal force would have thrown him to the other side of the cockpit and pinned him there. As it was, he could feel the straps cutting into his shoulders and hear them strain. He let himself absorb the thrill of the spin for a few seconds before he applied full right rudder and leveled the plane off. A glance down told him that he'd come out of the tailspin about one thousand feet above the ground.

Plenty of room to spare. He laughed and sent the plane climbing again.

A half hour later, it was with some regret that he headed the Cessna back to the airfield. A couple of spins was all he had time for today. That was the promise he'd made himself when he'd decided to take the plane up. But he was tempted…

No, he was not going to be late for his grandmother's seventy-fifth birthday party.

Then he grinned again. One more loop wouldn't break his promise. So with the airfield in sight, he completed one more for the road.

"YOU'RE BORED."

Nash Fortune didn't bother to deny the charge as he faced Maggie Fortune, the tiny dynamo of a woman he loved most in the world. They stood on the balcony that opened off of her office. Below them her birthday party was in full swing. While the sun splashed red across the horizon, guests sipped champagne and nibbled at canapés as they clustered in groups around the pool or strolled along a maze of paths. The buzz of conversation and laughter mixed with the muted sounds of a string quartet.

A few moments ago, he and his grandmother had been standing with his friends Jonah and Gabe and Nicola, Gabe's new fiancée, at the far end of the pool. They'd all been catching up with Father Mike, and without warning, his yawn had just escaped. He'd thought he'd hidden it, but his grandmother's eagle eye had caught it and she'd announced that she needed to steal him away for a moment.

"Well? Am I right?"

What could he say? She was.

She wagged a finger at him. "What worries me is you yawned just like that the night you set Captain Kirk and Mr. Spock loose in the middle of my dinner party."

He grinned at her. "You remember my gerbils' names?"

"Of course. One of my dinner guests fainted, I nearly lost the deal I was negotiating, and my chef quit because no one ate his main course. All because your pets got loose from the Starship Enterprise." Her eyes, green as the emeralds she wore in her ears, twinkled at him and her lips twitched now just as they had on that long ago evening.

Nash took her hands in his. "Grams, your birthday bash is safe. I promise I haven't brought any gerbils or other small animals with me."

"That isn't the only mischief you used to get into when you weren't challenged enough. Do you recall when you were in fourth grade and you glued poor Katie Lynn Peabody to her desk? And you put the snake you'd brought in for show and tell in your teacher's desk?"

"Surely the statute of limitations has run out on those crimes. How about if I apologize for yawning?"

"Why in hell should you apologize?" Maggie frowned at him.

"Because it's made you worry." He drew his grandmother into his arms and just held her for a moment. Maggie's hair was pure white now instead of the raven color it had once been. But it was styled to perfection, and in her red silk pantsuit she looked as if she'd just stepped off the cover of a women's fashion magazine.

Looks weren't her only asset. She had one of the sharpest minds he'd ever encountered. For the past two decades, she'd run Fortune Enterprises, a large business empire that ranged from mining and real estate holdings to publishing. And twenty-one years ago, she'd also taken over the job of raising him after his father's untimely death in the Gulf War.

As he drew back, Nash wondered which she'd claim was the bigger of the two challenges.

"Thanks for the hug," she said. "They've always been your best method of trying to distract me. But not tonight. I didn't bring you up here just to scold you because you yawned at my birthday party."

She tapped a finger on his chest. "The problem is you're bored, period. I can see the signs. You're not sleeping well."

That was true although he'd never figured out how his grandmother could always tell.

"More lines around your eyes," she said with her usual knack for reading his mind. "And twice so far this evening, I've seen you gaze off into space. Admit it. I was right. You're regretting your decision to request a teaching assignment at the Air Force Academy."

"Not true," he said.

She held a hand up. "Let me finish. After all, I was responsible for your decision."

"Partly responsible. Have you ever thought that I might have needed to come home? That maybe I was a bit restless and bored before I learned about your surgery?"

She stared at him for a moment.

Nash fully sympathized with her surprise. It was the first time he'd admitted to himself that his current feeling of…restlessness may have predated his teaching assignment. He might have been courting boredom even in Afghanistan.

She narrowed her eyes. "You've got the same problem your father had when he was about your age. Our country's wars are winding down. And you're getting older. You're starting to see that you can't fly those fighter planes forever. I imagine facing the young men and women who'll replace you in the classroom each day drives the point home even more sharply. So I'll tell you what I told your father. You can't stop time. You have to accept it and go with the flow."

He raised his brows.

Her lips twitched again. "I know. It's *my* milestone birthday we're celebrating, but your thirtieth wasn't that long ago. And you can't be a fly-boy forever. Your father was getting a bit bored with the life of a pilot in peace time before the Gulf War erupted."

Nash captured one of her hands in his again. As usual, she was spot-on about some of what he was feeling.

"You could always think of making a career change."

He met her eyes without disguising the surprise in his. From the time he'd been a child, she'd supported his dream of one day following in his father's footsteps and becoming a pilot in the Air Force. She'd never once put any kind of pressure on him to consider taking over one of the many companies she ran—in spite of the fact that when she'd lost his father, she'd lost the son she'd expected to one day fill her shoes.

He narrowed his eyes as a sudden thought occurred to him. "Something has changed. You've received some bad news from your doctors."

"No, nothing like that. I'm fine. I'd tell you in a heartbeat if I wasn't." Maggie raised the hand holding hers and patted it. "I'm just planting a seed about the future. It's my birthday. I have a right to plant seeds."

Nash laughed. "You have the right to plant seeds whenever you want." And they had a tendency to take root and grow. Johnny Appleseed had nothing on his grandmother in that department. But he was beginning to wonder just what seed she'd intended to plant when she'd brought him up here to the balcony.

Maggie continued to meet his gaze. "I also have a right to worry. And perhaps feel a bit guilty."

"Guilty? About what?"

"Your intolerance of boredom is probably embedded in a gene you've inherited directly from me. None of the Nashes were long on patience. And your impatience as a baby is how you came to be called by your middle name. When what you've inherited from my side of the family is mixed in with what you've inherited from the black sheep on the Fortune side of the family. Well?" She threw up her hands. "It's worrisome."

"You're not planning on giving me the Jeremiah Fortune lecture again?"

Her eyes widened. "You remember him, then?"

His eyes narrowed. "If you can call up the names of my pet gerbils, I can certainly remember Jeremiah's.

You were always lecturing me that if I didn't mend my ways, I'd grow up to be just like him instead of my father. I also remember that when I sassed you by asking just how badly a Fortune heir could turn out, you filled me in on my ancestor's untimely and grim demise."

Maggie remembered every detail of what she'd told him. The story was a good one, and she'd used it ruthlessly. Jeremiah had been the younger brother of Nash's great-great-great-grandfather, the first Thaddeus. Though the details were sketchy, the story had the drama of a soap opera. After the two Fortune brothers had settled in Colorado and discovered a rich vein of gold, they'd argued over a woman. Tradition held that Thaddeus had won the woman and Jeremiah had run off to prospect for more gold on his own. Two years later he'd been hanged as a horse thief.

"Time to come clean, Grams," Nash said. "You didn't call me up here to remind me that I might have a few genes from a black sheep in my DNA. What's the real reason?"

Out of the corner of her eye, Maggie saw the real reason making her way across the terrace below them. Bianca Quinn had arrived right on schedule. Even now, Father Mike was raising his hand in greeting. Thank heavens Nash wasn't looking out at the party anymore. Because she hadn't finished yet. "I want a favor."

"Anything."

"I've hired a writer and commissioned her to write a book on the history of the Fortune family. There'll be an emphasis on the early years, but she's going to chronicle the entire saga right up to the present."

She noted surprise flicker in his eyes, then curiosity.

"Aren't you nervous about dragging all of the skeletons out of the closet?"

Maggie laughed. "I think it should prove highly amusing. Scandals sell."

"I'm assuming you checked out this writer's credentials."

"Not to worry. I had your friend Gabe run a thorough background check. And she's good. Her first book made the *Times* extended book list."

"It sounds like you're right on top of everything, as usual. How can I help?"

She beamed a smile at him. "I want you to cooperate fully with her. She'll want to interview you as the current Fortune heir and one of Denver's most eligible bachelors. And she's been away from Denver for a while. I just want you to make her feel as comfortable as possible while she's settling in to work on the project. Be nice to her."

Maggie was careful to keep her expression bland, but she hadn't raised a fool. Nash knew that she was up to something. She also figured that by now Bianca had joined Father Mike and Nash's friends at the far end of the pool. So it was nearly time.

"You're worrying me, Grams. Just how ugly is she? And even if she were, why would you think I wouldn't be nice to her?"

"Because the woman I've hired to write the Fortune family saga is Bianca Quinn. She's just arrived and she's joined your friends."

Nash whipped his gaze back to the group he and his grandmother had left earlier at the far end of the pool. His eyes fastened on her immediately. A tall blonde, slim as a wand in a white sundress. Though her back was to him, recognition instantly flooded his system. So did the memories. Feelings he'd buried long ago shot to the surface. A mix of love, desire, anger and hurt froze him to the spot.

Unable to move, he absorbed the long slender legs, the narrow waist, the honey-colored hair that fell to her shoulders. He'd known every inch of her and he hadn't forgotten a single detail. She matched perfectly with the image that he hadn't been aware he still carried in his mind.

What the hell was it doing there?

Then, as if she were aware of his gaze on her, she turned and glanced up at the balcony. Like a two-fisted punch to the gut, he felt desire, hot and raw. Not a memory, this time. The real thing.

Then he couldn't think at all. It was as if no time at all had passed. The impulse to go to her was so strong. He wasn't aware until he felt the warmth of Maggie's hands on one of his that he'd gripped the balcony railing.

Glancing down, he noted the whiteness of his knuckles. What had been his plan? To just leap onto the terrace and run to her?

No way. Time had passed. He wasn't a nineteen-year-old anymore. Nash drew in a deep breath and let it out. No other woman had ever affected him the way Bianca Quinn had. Evidently, she still could.

He drew in another breath. He was older now. And he knew a lot more about women than he had at nineteen.

So he'd handle her. For his grandmother's sake. But it wasn't his promise to his grandmother that kept his eyes lingering on Bianca. Without thinking he touched a finger to his chest just where the medal lay beneath his uniform. He'd find a way to handle her.

Turning to Maggie, he smiled. "I'll be happy to give her an interview. Why don't we join the party?"

2

Five minutes earlier...

WITH NERVELESS FINGERS, Bianca Quinn handed the keys of her car over to the valet.

"Welcome to Fortune Mansion, Miss Quinn."

At her surprised look, he smiled. "Ms. Fortune said you'd be arriving right about now. She asked us to keep an eye out for you. Just follow the lighted path around the side of the house. The party's in the garden and you're in plenty of time for the birthday cake. Enjoy."

Enjoy. Maybe she could once she got through this first meeting with Nash Fortune. The path was only a few feet to her right, and she could hear the sound of laughter and the faint strains of Vivaldi. But for a moment she simply couldn't make herself move.

She'd read about déjà vu, but she'd never before realized the physical impact it might have. For just an instant she felt transported back in time to that fateful day eleven years ago when she'd stood on this very spot. She'd sensed then that her life was about to change.

It had.

And she felt the same way now.

As ridiculous as it was, she couldn't immediately shake off the feeling, nor could she seem to drag her gaze away from the Fortune Mansion's stone and glass facade.

But she would no longer allow it to intimidate her. The new bargain she'd struck with Maggie Fortune was entirely different from the one she'd made eleven years ago when she'd promised to disappear from Nash Fortune's life. The new one was strictly business. She was going to research and write a history of the Fortune family in Colorado.

A family saga wasn't the type of book she usually wrote. And as lucrative as Maggie's offer was, she would have turned it down if it hadn't been for two things. First, she was intrigued by the story, sketchy as it was, of the two Fortune brothers who'd discovered gold in the 1860s and started a dynasty. She had a gut feeling that if she just dug a little deeper, she would find something, and her hunches were seldom wrong.

Her second reason for accepting Maggie's deal was one that the woman had pointed out to her—she could kill two birds with one stone. She had to come to the Denver area anyway to begin seriously researching her latest true crime book—the real story behind the disappearance of Cadet Brian Silko from the Air Force Academy more than a decade ago. Just as she had with her first book, she would visit the scene of the crime, so to speak—in this case, the Air Force Academy in Colorado Springs.

Not that she was sure a crime had been committed. But she had a strong hunch that there had been some kind of cover-up. And it might still be going on. When she'd called the superintendent of the Air Force Academy to ask for an interview concerning Brian's disappearance, he'd refused to even speak with her on the phone. In her experience, when someone didn't want to talk, it was because they had something to hide.

And the person who'd sent her the three anonymous notes agreed.

She hadn't thought of Brian Silko in years. Not until two months ago when she'd been doing a book-signing in a Barnes & Noble in Chicago. Out of the corner of her eye, she'd seen a tall young woman with dark hair slip a note under a pile of her books. The message had been concise: "For your next book, why don't you find out the true story behind Cadet Brian Silko's disappearance from the Air Force Academy eleven years ago?"

Of course, she'd recognized the name right away. Brian had been a year ahead of her in junior high and she'd interviewed him for an article in the school newspaper. It was right before his family had moved to Phoenix. Her story had focused on Brian's love of flying and his dream of one day attending the Air Force Academy.

Brian Silko had achieved his dream. He'd been in Nash's class their freshman year at the academy. They'd both played for the Falcons, the academy's football team. Then in the spring, Brian had stolen a small plane from the airfield and completely vanished.

It had been all over the news. She and Nash had talked about it, of course, but they'd been too involved with each other to pay much notice. No one had discovered why Brian had done what he'd done. And no one had ever found him or the wreckage of the plane.

The second anonymous note, postmarked from Denver, had been sent to her editor a few days later. He'd urged her to at least do some preliminary research. But she'd already started on that. Brian's mother had died a year ago, and she'd hadn't been able to locate his sister yet. What she'd found in the press coverage hadn't been anything more than she'd known at the time. No one seemed to know why Brian had suddenly stolen that plane or where he might have gone. And within a month, the press had forgotten about him.

So had she for over a decade.

Bianca had been well and truly hooked when the third note arrived bearing the postmark of the Air Force Academy in Colorado Springs—it stated that Brian was alive. If that was true, why hadn't he been found or come forward? And what had made him give up his dream of graduating from the Air Force Academy? There was a story here all right, and she was going to start by locating the people who'd known Brian the year he'd disappeared. One of those people was Nash Fortune.

And you're afraid to see him again.

Bianca drew in a deep breath and let it out. She was being ridiculous. She had nothing to fear from Nash Fortune because she was no longer that naive seventeen-year-old girl who could be completely swept away by what she felt for a man. Nor was she that young girl with a dream of one day becoming a published writer.

She was a writer. "A top-rate investigative journalist," one of her reviews had read. Her first book, *Cover Up,* had made the *Times* extended list and her publisher had already accepted the proposal for her second book on Brian Silko.

Straightening her shoulders, she shifted her gaze to the path leading to the garden. All she had to do was focus on her work. Nash's current teaching assignment at the Air Force Academy could prove to be very helpful. At the very least, he could share his insights into the kind of person Brian had been. And like his grandmother, Nash could open doors for her by putting her in contact with others at the academy who might know something. What had happened between them had ended long ago. Water under the bridge. He'd certainly forgiven her by now for running away.

Perhaps he'd even forgotten her. They'd been young and foolish and totally unsuited for one another. Her Aunt Molly, the woman who'd raised her from the time she'd been orphaned at the age of three, had been a cleaning woman at the St. Francis Center for Boys. Nash Fortune had been the grandson of one of the richest women in the United States.

But you haven't forgotten him, nagged that little voice again.

Maybe not. Nash had been her first love. A woman always remembered her first. There was the guilt factor, too. She'd been the one to call things off. She was the one who'd run away.

That was why she was making the whole thing into a mountain—and Nash would be viewing it as a molehill. Surely, now that they were both adults who were living their dreams, he would see that she'd made the right decision.

Still, she'd taken money for what she'd done. She might not have signed the papers and taken Maggie's check if Father Mike Flynn hadn't been there standing at the older woman's side. And they'd made it so easy for her. All she had to do was leave a note for Nash near the statue of St. Francis in the little prayer garden at the center.

And it wasn't just money Maggie had offered her. It had been an acceptance letter from a college in the Boston area where she could major in writing. There'd also been a job for her Aunt Molly in one of Maggie's companies that had a branch office in Cambridge. Maggie Fortune was as skillful as the serpent in Eden when it came to offering the right bait.

Bianca fisted her hands at her sides. Bribe or not, she'd been right to do what she'd done. She'd gone off to college and Nash had been able to continue at the Air Force Academy without the burden of a teenage wife in Denver.

No matter that it had hurt so much at the time. Nor that there was a little place in her heart that still ached.

The important thing was that they'd both achieved their dreams and might not have if she hadn't made that bargain eleven years ago.

So what are you so afraid of?

Good question.

She pressed a hand to her stomach and willed her nerves to settle. She had a plan. She'd arrived in Denver two days ago, settled herself in a hotel, and even visited the Colorado Springs Police Department to look over their files on the Silko disappearance. Tonight's meeting with Nash was just another step. She'd set up an interview with him and use the time to probe his relationship with Brian as well as his position as the sole heir to the Fortune riches.

A few days from now she was going to laugh about what a non-issue meeting him again had turned out to be.

Stepping away from the willow tree, she strode down the path toward the laughter and the music. The important thing was to find out what had really happened to Cadet Brian Silko and write his story.

The moment she stepped onto the flagstone terrace, Bianca paused to scan the crowd. She had to hand it to Maggie Fortune. The woman knew how to throw a party. At the far end of the pool, she caught a glimpse of the musicians, and she thought they'd switched to Mozart. But it was hard to tell above the laughter and conversation.

White-jacketed waiters carrying trays of fluted glasses cut paths through the clusters of guests. She spotted a senior state senator whose name frequently made the news. She was pretty sure she recognized an aging film star she'd had a crush on when she was thirteen, and there were at least two men who'd retired from hosting network evening news.

"Miss Quinn?"

Bianca turned to a tall, very distinguished-looking man at her side. She guessed him to be in his early seventies. He had gray, thinning hair, and in his perfectly tailored gray suit, he reminded her of the actor Walter Pigeon, who'd appeared in the original *Thin Man* movies.

"I'm Grady, Ms. Fortune's house manager. She's stepped inside for a moment and she asked me to greet you in her place. You'll find Father Flynn and some other people you might remember over on the other side of the pool."

"Thank you." Bianca started to thread her way in the direction that Grady had pointed, but it took her a few moments before she spotted Father Mike. The instant he saw her, he smiled and waved. At once, something inside of her eased.

She'd originally met him through her Aunt Molly. On Saturdays, she'd frequently helped her aunt to clean the St. Francis Center. At the end of her junior year in high school, Father Mike had offered her the job of writing the newsletter for the center. It had been her first official writing job, and she could never thank him enough for the opportunity.

Working on the newsletter had also given her the opportunity to get to know him, and he was the kindest and most truly holy person she'd ever met. He'd even taken the time to fly east to visit her and her aunt during the first few years she'd been in college. And when her aunt had passed on two years ago, he'd flown in to say the funeral mass.

As Bianca began to weave her way toward him, she shifted her gaze to the people he was with. That was all it took to set her nerves dancing again. The pretty young woman was a stranger, but in spite of the passage of time, she recognized the two men immediately. Gabe Wilder and Jonah Stone had been Nash's best friends at the St. Francis Center.

Gabe wore black. That had been his favorite color in high school, but the shirts hadn't been silk back then. But Jonah's clothes also had her taking a second look. He'd been a jeans-and-T-shirt kind of boy, but the suit he was wearing today had been tailored to fit his tall, lanky frame perfectly, and she was pretty sure it boasted a designer label. He definitely wasn't the rough-edged street kid she remembered.

As she drew closer, Father Mike held out his arms and she walked right into them.

"Welcome back," he murmured. "You must come and visit me soon so we can catch up."

"I will," she promised as he released her. It was at that precise moment she felt the hairs on the back of her neck spring to attention.

Nash.

She could feel the heat of his gaze on her skin, and the moment she turned her head, she saw him. He stood next to his grandmother on a balcony overlooking the terrace and pool. Her heart started to pound, her breath caught in her throat. He was tall and blond and just as handsome as the image she'd had in her mind all these years.

The fact that he was wearing his uniform did nothing at all to lessen the intensity of his effect on her senses. But it wasn't until she met his eyes that she felt the full impact. Everything inside of her heated as her mind emptied and simply filled with him. Pleasure shot through her, along with the beginnings of that same primitive and urgent desire she'd felt for him all those years ago.

With it came the impulse to forget every thing else and just go to him. She was not naturally impulsive, but he'd always had that effect on her, making her want to toss the world away and go into freefall just to be with him. He still had the power to make her feel that way. Baffled, she fought hard to keep her feet firmly planted where they were. But she might have lost the battle if he hadn't chosen that moment to turn to his grandmother.

Even then, it took all of her concentration to turn her own head and focus as Father Mike said, "You must remember Gabe and Jonah."

"Yes." The word was barely audible and Bianca reminded herself to smile.

"Welcome back to Denver," Gabe said.

Jonah merely nodded.

In spite of the friendliness of Gabe's words, cool wariness was what she saw in the eyes of both men. Of course, both of them had been close to Nash when she'd run out on him. Clearly, they hadn't forgotten. But when Father Mike introduced her to Gabe's fiancée, Nicola

Guthrie, the young woman's handshake was warm, her smile genuine. "Are you the Bianca Quinn who wrote *Cover Up?*"

"I am."

"What a delight to meet you. Gabe mentioned he knew you when I starting raving about your book."

"Nicola's a true fan of your investigative technique," Gabe said.

"I was going to write you a letter," Nicola said. "I told my father that we ought to recruit you to work for the FBI."

"I'm a researcher and a writer, not a crime fighter," Bianca said.

"We could still benefit from your skills." Nicola turned to Jonah. "You have to read *Cover Up.* It all takes place in this little town in upstate New York, not far from Cornell University. The last place you'd expect there would be a home invasion and grisly murders. And the police solved it in record time—or they thought they had. One suspect was shot to death by the police, the other tried, convicted and sentenced to jail. The real killer would have gotten away if Bianca hadn't decided to write about it."

Nicola turned back to Bianca. "How did you come to choose that particular story?"

"Someone brought it to my attention when I attended a conference in the area, and I got a feeling, a hunch, that there was a story there."

"I knew you'd make a good agent. Following hunches is essential in good investigative work."

Jonah turned to Bianca. "What brings you back to Denver?"

It didn't surprise Bianca one bit that Jonah was the one to ask that question. He'd let her know eleven years ago that he hadn't approved of her relationship with Nash. The rough kid from the streets was territorial when it came to his friends, and he never believed in beating around the bush.

"I'm working on two projects."

"True crime again?" Nicola asked.

"One of them is." Though her back was turned, she could sense that Nash and his grandmother were approaching. The tingle of awareness moved through every cell in her body. She wasn't sure how she managed it, but she kept her eyes on Nicola. "But I'm also here at the request of Mrs. Fortune. She's commissioned me to write the history of the Fortune family."

"Indeed I have," Maggie said as she and Nash joined the group. "I've just been telling Nash, and I think he's a bit nervous about pulling all the family skeletons out of the closet."

Bianca barely had time to turn when Nash took her hands in his and leaned down to touch his lips to her cheek. She felt the imprint of each one of his fingers on hers as if they were a brand. The brush of his mouth on her skin was brief, a simple social contact, but her heart skipped a beat, then raced.

"Bianca, it's wonderful to see you again," he said. "You're even lovelier than I remembered."

He released her in the time it took her to meet his eyes. All she read in his was the warmth one might expect to see in the eyes of an old and dear friend. Nothing that came close to matching the flash of heat his touch had ignited.

"Good to see you, too," she managed to say, and wondered that her nose didn't grow like Pinocchio's for telling the lie. There was no way that her reaction to seeing Nash Fortune again was *good*. Even after he'd released her hands, she'd wanted badly to throw her arms around him.

She wasn't the girl she'd been at seventeen—so willing and eager to toss caution to the winds. She was no longer Juliet to his Romeo. What was wrong with her? She was an adult, for heaven's sake.

But for a few minutes the conversation around her was just a buzz of noise, and she simply couldn't pick up the thread.

It's the Nash Effect, the little voice said.

She couldn't argue with that assessment. She was so aware of him standing near her. It was as if her entire body remembered him. And recalled his touch. When he laughed at something Gabe said, the sound rippled along her nerve endings.

It wasn't until he stepped closer to Gabe and Jonah that she felt her brain cells click on. She had a story to research, she reminded herself again.

Two stories. In a few more seconds, she'd even remember what they were. Bubbles of panic erupted and cleared her brain. Now, if she could just stop looking at him.

"Are you all right, dear?"

Father Mike. Gratefully, she turned to face him. "I will be."

"Yes." He took her hand in his and patted it. "You will be."

How often had he said those words to her before? The first time had been when she'd worked on the first newsletter for the St. Francis Center. She'd been so nervous about seeing something she'd written in print for the first time. Father Mike had taken her into the small prayer garden tucked in between the center and a basketball court. A statue of St. Francis sat on a dais in the small space, and he'd told her that saying a prayer to the statue would help.

It had. But so had Father Mike's calm belief in her, then and over the years. She would be all right this time, too.

When she turned back to the others, she could finally follow what they were saying. And she could look at other people besides Nash. The men were discussing an upcoming basketball tournament at the Boys and Girls Club and settling on a poker night since Jonah was in town. Their easy camaraderie matched perfectly with her memories of the three of them.

"I know that you're busy," Nicola said to her. "But I'd love to get together with you for lunch?"

Bianca smiled at her. "I'd love that."

"I'll call you," Nicola said before she turned to respond to something Gabe had said.

When a passing waiter offered a flute of champagne, she took one. On the bright side, she'd discovered the answer to one question. Nash was definitely not going to be a non-issue for her. Because he stood in profile, his attention focused on what Gabe was saying, she was able to study him objectively for the first time. His face was leaner, the laugh lines more pronounced. His body was still tall and lanky, but it looked harder. His hands had certainly seemed harder, too, in the moment they'd clasped hers.

They'll feel different on your skin when he makes love to you.

Bianca took a sip of her champagne. She was just not going to allow herself to go there. Second thing on the bright side—what she was feeling was one-sided. He hadn't glanced at her since he'd moved away. The fact that he seemed to be treating her as an old friend was a good thing. She'd find a way to handle her feelings. She was older now. And she could still use his help with both her projects. When she interviewed him as the current heir to the Fortune dynasty, she'd also ask him about Brian. They'd been classmates. At the very least, he could provide deeper insights into the kind of person Brian had been. At best, he could save her a lot of time by putting her in touch with others who'd known Brian personally that year. She just had to keep her focus.

"Having second thoughts?"

Bianca turned to see Maggie stood next to her. She met the older woman's eyes. "No."

"Good." Maggie took her free hand and gave it a quick squeeze. "How did your visit to the Colorado Springs Police Department go?"

Bianca smiled at her. "Very smoothly, thanks to you. Mayor DeBlois sends you his best. The sergeant there had the files on Brian Silko's disappearance all ready for me to read. Unfortunately, I didn't discover anything new. The detective who did the investigation has retired. No one seemed to know his current address. My next move will be to locate him. But first, I intend to get started on the book you're paying me for."

"Good. But I knew when I convinced you to take on the scandalous Fortunes that you were also here to research your next book. You're free to juggle your work load any way you see fit. I'll be out of town for a few days, but I've arranged with Grady, my house manager, for you to have access to the library and the family archives whenever you wish. He has instructions to let you in and out—at any hour."

"I'll start tomorrow."

"Good."

"Maggie, sorry I'm late. Happy birthday."

"James." Maggie turned to hug the man who wore a dress uniform that matched Nash's.

"General." Nash nodded at the man.

Maggie introduced General James Winslow to the group. When it was her turn, Bianca grasped the hand the general extended. She was a little surprised when the current superintendent of the Air Force Academy showed no sign of recognition. It had been less than a month since he'd refused to meet with her or even speak to her on the phone. After that, she'd received the same refusal from everyone else she'd phoned. No one wanted to talk about Cadet Brian Silko.

There was a story to uncover, all right.

When the string quartet segued from Brahms to a lively rendition of "Happy Birthday," Maggie laughed. "I think that's a hint that I should cut my birthday cake."

As the group was dispersing in the direction of the cake, Bianca drew in a deep breath. She had a plan to complete before Nash drifted away. Taking a step toward him, she said, "I'd like to set up an appointment for an interview."

When he met her eyes, she could read nothing in them. "Grams told me as much. Are you free tomorrow morning around eleven?"

"Yes."

"I'll be in my office at the academy. Do you have transportation?"

She nodded. "A rental car."

"Then I'll have someone meet you at the main gate and show you the way."

"See you then." As Bianca watched him move ahead to fall into step with his grandmother and General Winslow, she thought she'd handled that well.

He could still arouse feelings in her, but she would

deal with them. She would just have to keep their relationship on a professional level.

As everyone burst into "Happy Birthday," she settled her gaze on Nash again. And her heart bounced hard and high. She might just as well have been seventeen again.

Keeping things professional will be a good trick if you can pull it off.

Bianca had no comeback for that.

3

NASH MADE ONE LAST crease in the paper airplane he'd been crafting for the past fifteen minutes. Creating them had been a habit he'd picked up from his dad. They used to sit side by side for hours at the kitchen table in his grandmother's house completing entire combat squadrons and then waging war. As a result of years of practice, Nash had learned to make an aeronautically superior paper plane. Usually the process helped to clear his mind and even solve problems.

And he definitely had a problem.

Hefting his latest masterpiece between his finger and thumb, he launched it with one practiced flick of his wrist. It soared upward for two seconds before it nose dived onto the floor nearly a foot short of its intended target—his wastebasket.

Glancing over the top of his desk, Nash noted that it was the fifth plane that had crashed before reaching its destination. In the past hour, only one of his master-pieces had survived the trip.

And the failed missions littering his office floor were all due to Bianca Quinn.

Rising, he shoved his hands into his pockets and

paced through the debris to the window of his office. In the distance, mountain peaks jutted into a cloudless blue sky. After eleven years, she was back in his life, and he wasn't at all sure how it would play out. He wasn't sure how he wanted it to play out.

He felt the same way about her now as he had when he'd first seen her eleven years ago. He'd gotten a glimmer of that feeling when he'd first seen her from his grandmother's balcony, but taking her hands and kissing her cheek had confirmed it.

Nash found the strength to smile. He'd wanted to throw her over his shoulder and simply leave the party. And it might have been worth it to see the expression on his grandmother's face.

Because Maggie Fortune was pulling strings in this situation. He had no doubt of that. But his more compelling problem was Bianca. What he'd learned last night was that he wanted her, intensely, urgently, to the exclusion of everything else. Just as he had the first time.

How could that possibly be? Time had intervened. He was older now. So was she. But all he'd had to do was see her, meet her gaze, and she'd sent him into the same tailspin she had the first time.

What had happened between them in their teens, as intense as it had been, should have been over. More than a decade had passed. And it was the "to the exclusion of everything else" part that was the most worrisome. At nineteen, he could understand it.

Now… With a frown, he paced back to his desk and sat down. There was a lot in both their lives that couldn't be excluded. And there was so much they didn't know about each other.

He hadn't even been aware that she'd written a book.

He glanced at his computer screen and reread the review he'd pulled up. "Gripping…a first-rate page-turner."

Unable to resist, he'd downloaded a free chapter, and the voice, the energy in the writing had immediately captivated him. He could hear her, feel her in the words. And the story was a fascinating one.

On the surface, the slaughter of an ordinary middle-class family in a presumably safe neighborhood in Dryden, New York, had all the markings of a random home invasion. The suspects, a woman and her son, had been tracked down when they'd run up charges on credit cards that had been stolen from the victims. The son had been killed by the police, and though the woman had never confessed, she'd been convicted by the fingerprint evidence at the scene of the multiple murders.

Fingerprint evidence that Bianca Quinn had later discovered had been planted by an overzealous member of the state police. Thanks to her diligent investigation of the cold case file and her extensive interviews, another suspect had surfaced and had been arrested.

It didn't surprise Nash at all that Bianca was coming into her own as a published author. Writing had always been her first love, and it had motivated her decision to cancel their elopement plans and leave Denver.

Though it had hurt like hell at the time, Nash knew what it was to pursue a dream. He'd been equally focused on his future career in the Air Force. At nineteen, he'd been convinced that they could each achieve their goals while they were together. In the end he'd had to accept that Bianca's love of writing had prevailed over her love of him. She'd made that quite clear in the "Dear John" note she'd left him at the base of the statue of St. Francis.

Anger, bafflement, hurt. He'd experienced all of them

the night he'd read her note. His first impulse had been to go after her and convince her that she was wrong. And if that hadn't worked, he would have simply dragged her back. That had been his battle strategy until Father Mike had walked into the prayer garden. The priest had talked to him in that calm, logical way of his and persuaded him to see everything from Bianca's point of view.

Father Mike had been honest with him about his grandmother's involvement, and about the opportunities she'd opened up for Bianca—a college education, a chance to major in writing at a prestigious Ivy League school—opportunities that Nash couldn't offer at that point in his life. In the end, Father Mike had gotten a promise from him to let some time go by before he did anything rash. Then holding his hand, the priest had encouraged him to say a prayer to the statue. If his memory served him correctly, he'd prayed what was in his heart, that Bianca would change her mind and come back to him. But she hadn't.

End of story. He'd had a heart-to-heart with his grandmother, but she'd used the same argument as Father Mike had. If he truly loved Bianca, he'd give her this chance. So he hadn't gone after her. The pain he'd felt all those years ago had eventually faded. The wounds had healed.

Then he'd seen her at his grandmother's birthday party and felt as if he'd been struck by a thunderbolt, one that had opened up everything he'd believed he'd buried long ago.

He glanced at his watch. In fifteen minutes she was going to walk through the door of his office for an interview. And he wanted her as much as he'd wanted her before, and more than he'd ever wanted any other woman.

And that was enough to give any sane man pause. He was no stranger to going with impulse. He enjoyed taking risks. That part of his nature was what made him a good pilot. But on a mission, he always weighed the consequences of various strategies before hand.

Eleven years ago, he hadn't done that with Bianca. He'd been too blindsided by her. He'd rushed into a relationship with her with very little thought of the future— his, hers or theirs. And when they'd gotten around to a plan, it hadn't worked out.

He threaded his fingers behind his head and leaned back in his chair. Hell, he knew a lot about battle strategies. First you had to have a goal. And he thought he had that. What he was feeling for her was not going to go away. He wanted to taste her again. He wanted her again.

He picked up a piece of paper and began folding it. There was no denying the fact that she was special to him. And it wasn't just impulse or raging hormones driving him now. He was curious about the woman she'd become. Having read some of her work, he was even more intrigued.

What he needed was an effective strategy for reaching his goal. One that considered her as well as himself. The problem was, he wasn't quite sure what that strategy was. He'd have to figure it out. He lifted the paper plane and flicked his wrist a few times. He'd weigh the data as it came in and adjust. With a grin, he aimed the airplane at his wastebasket and let it rip. Then he watched it ricochet off the edge and nose dive to the floor.

"I remember when your father used to make paper planes. I swear he'd make twenty or thirty of them before he flew each mission."

Startled, Nash rose to greet General Winslow. "Come in, sir."

"I can also remember the days when you called me Uncle Jimmy."

"A long time ago." Winslow was medium height with the compact build of a boxer. He'd roomed with Nash's father when they'd gone through the Air Force Academy together, and they'd served together in the Gulf War. In the first year or two after his father had died, the general had visited his grandmother frequently. But until Nash had come back to the Air Force Academy to teach, he hadn't seen Winslow in years. And it was the first time since he'd returned that the general had paid him a visit in his office.

"Was there something you wanted to talk to me about?" Nash asked.

Winslow studied him for a moment before he spoke. "I overheard you inviting Bianca Quinn here to your office this morning. How much do you know about her?"

The question surprised Nash, but he managed not to let it show. "She's a writer and she wants to interview me because my grandmother has hired her to write a book about the Fortune family."

The general nodded. "I'm sure that Maggie has checked her out and knows that she's a journalist with a flair for digging up secrets."

Nash smiled. "I think she's looking forward to having some of the Fortune family's secrets made public."

Winslow smiled in response, but his eyes remained serious. For a moment, the silence stretched between them.

"Is there a problem?" Nash finally asked. There had to be something that had prompted the general's visit.

Was he worried about the book his grandmother had hired Bianca to write? Nash couldn't imagine James Winslow playing a role in any of the dirty laundry that might be aired. He'd had a stellar career in the Air Force, and his association with Nash's family stemmed from a close friendship with his father that had ended more than twenty years ago.

"I'm not sure. I didn't want to say anything to your grandmother last night in the middle of her party. But I recognized Quinn's name the instant I was introduced to her. Are you sure writing a biography of your family is all this Quinn woman has come here to do?"

"As far as I know. What do you know that I don't?"

Winslow sighed. "A month ago, she called my office several times and she also bothered other members of the faculty. She wanted to set up interviews for a book she's writing on the disappearance of Cadet Brian Silko. I had my administrative assistant turn her down and request that she stop calling."

"Why?"

The general's brows rose. "As superintendent, I have to look out for the best interests of the school. You must remember the Silko case and what a sensation it made in the press. You knew Brian Silko."

"Not well. We were on the football team together freshman year. He was a kicker, a good one."

"And you were an excellent quarterback. I caught one or two of your games when I visited family in the area. I was here in the spring when Silko went missing. I witnessed the press coverage."

After rising, the general walked to the window and gazed out. "At 7:00 a.m. on February 2, Cadet Brian Silko stole the commandant's privately owned Cessna from its hangar here on our flight field and disappeared with it. Never to be found. He left no note, no explanation. He'd talked to no one about his plans. There was no evidence that he'd been taken against his will. No ransom note had ever been delivered. He simply vanished. The Air Force and the Colorado Springs police conducted separate investigations, and they reached the same conclusion. He stole a plane and disappeared of his own free will."

"And when he never surfaced, everyone assumed that he crashed the plane in some remote area," Nash said. It had all happened during the spring semester when he and Bianca had fallen desperately in love. Of course, they'd read about the case and talked about it some, but they'd been so involved with each other.

"Exactly." The general turned back to face him.

But neither the plane nor Cadet Silko had ever been found. Gradually, the story had faded from everyone's memory. Nash hadn't thought of it in years.

"And you've paid me this visit because you suspect that Bianca Quinn's reason for coming to Denver might be to research Silko's disappearance as well as my ancestors' colorful pasts."

"Exactly," the general said again. "And the official position of the Air Force Academy is that the case is closed. We have no comment. If she presses you, I'd like your word to restate that position very clearly to Ms. Quinn."

"You have it," Nash said without hesitation. And when the general rose, he stood up and remained standing until the general left.

He'd have no trouble giving Bianca the official position of the Air Force Academy. But he was pretty sure he wasn't going to comply with the subtext of the general's wishes now that his curiosity had been well and truly stirred up. First of all, the general had used the phrase "digging up secrets" when he'd first talked about Bianca's job. Were there some secrets surrounding the disappearance of Cadet Silko?

And what were Bianca's secrets? What exactly was it that had piqued her interest in Silko's disappearance after all these years? And why had she really come back to Denver?

Sitting back down at his desk, he glanced at his watch. Bianca wasn't due for another five minutes or so. But he was certain of one thing. If Bianca wanted his help, he was going to give it to her. What better chance to get to know her better and collect data? And if that meant he was playing with fire? So much the better. He grinned. This time when he shot the plane, it accomplished its mission.

He wasn't so sure where his plan would take him, or how often he'd have to modify his strategy, but as a pilot he'd learned long ago, the challenge was often more than half of the fun.

"CAPTAIN FORTUNE'S OFFICE is on the first floor," the young cadet said. "Right inside the entrance, take the corridor to your left and follow it around to Room 115."

"Thanks." Bianca smiled and waved at the young man as he drove off in his jeep. He'd met her at the front gates, provided her with a map of the entire campus, and explained that since they were in summer sessions, the campus wouldn't be as crowded as usual. Then she'd followed him to a parking lot at the side of Nash's building. On their way they'd driven past a parade field and the chapel with its spires reaching into an almost cloudless blue sky. Here and there, she'd spotted tour groups that appeared to be prospective students and their parents touring the campus.

Nash's building was a two-story structure with tinted glass windows that bounced back the sun's rays. She'd just locked her car when she saw General James Winslow exit the building through the double glass doors. He walked straight to a jeep that was waiting for him, and drove off.

She felt the same ripple of wariness she'd felt the night before when he'd shaken her hand at Maggie Fortune's birthday. A quick glance at the map her escort had given her indicated that this building did not house the superintendent's offices.

Still, he could have a perfectly good reason for visiting here this morning—something that had nothing to do with Nash or with her pending visit. But as she walked through the doors and turned down the corridor, she was confident that she'd made the right decision about at least one thing during the night. She was going to be honest with Nash about her interest in the disappearance of Brian Silko. And she was going to tell him everything about why she'd run away eleven years ago.

She owed him the truth about taking money from his grandmother even if it jeopardized getting his help with her stories.

Other than that, she hadn't decided how she was going to handle the fact that she was still intensely attracted to him. Thinking about him and what she'd felt when he'd touched her again had interfered with her sleep. And there was a part of her—a part that she couldn't seem to control—that was looking forward to seeing him again.

It had been years since she'd made wardrobe selections with a man in mind—eleven years, in fact. But she'd changed her clothes three times and her hairstyle twice. All because of Nash.

She wasn't a teenager in love and in lust for the first time. She was a grown woman with a goal. She was here to find out what caused Brian Silko to steal that plane and give up everything he'd worked so hard to achieve. And if he was alive, she was going to find him and let him tell his own story.

There was a good chance Nash could help her achieve her goal. That's all that she should be thinking about. She spotted his office the moment she took the first right turn in the corridor. Though she couldn't see him, she caught the flight of the paper airplane as it sailed through the open doorway and cruised to a rough landing a few feet away.

As she stooped over to pick it up, silly memories came flooding back. He'd taught her how to make them, but his had always sailed farther, and she'd never learned how to make them do a loop before they crashed. Sometimes he'd written her notes on his.

When she reached the fallen paper, she scooped it up and unfolded it. "Welcome back to Denver."

Her pulse pounded, her breath quickened even as something around her heart tightened. He was being kind. How was he going to feel about her when she told him the truth? About everything.

She glanced up to see that he was standing in the open doorway of his office, smiling at her with that same reckless gleam in his eyes that had caught her attention the first time she'd ever seen him.

He strode toward her, took her hand and pulled her down the corridor. "We're going for a ride."

4

"I THOUGHT WE WERE MEETING in your office." Bianca tucked the paper airplane into her bag as Nash hurried her along to the parking lot.

"Change of plan. Here, put this on."

She stared dubiously first at the sleek, black motorcycle and then at the helmet he held out to her. "We could take my car."

"Much less fun."

She met his eyes, saw the laughter and the challenge, and something inside of her melted. "I came here to interview you. I can hardly do it on a—what is this—a Harley?"

"Good eye. And I know a perfect spot for an interview—one where we won't be interrupted."

Although tempted, Bianca tried to hold on to common sense.

"How long has it been since you've seen the countryside on a motorcycle?"

She eyed the bike dubiously. "I've never been on one of those in my life."

"That's the best reason in the world for giving it a

try. It's the closest thing to flying without leaving the ground. C'mon. Just for the fun of it."

She met his eyes again, and the laughter, the promise of fun, had her donning the helmet and climbing on behind him. Then she recalled how much it was like Nash to do this to her—to just sweep her up in something he'd planned. But she couldn't blame it all on him. She'd always been game to go along with him just as she was doing right now. She hadn't even bothered to ask where they were going.

Any opportunity for further conversation became problematic as Nash started the bike and pulled out of the parking lot. She rested her hands lightly on his hips as they headed toward the entrance gates. As soon as they rode through them, he kicked the speed up on the bike and she held on more tightly.

They'd gone less than a mile when Bianca realized she *was* having fun. She liked the wind in her face and against her skin. It seemed to be blowing all of the worries and cares out of her mind.

Then there was the kick of adrenaline each time Nash pushed the bike into another burst of speed. For the first time since she'd left the party the night before, she let herself stop thinking and trying to plan. She just gave herself over to the moment.

How long had it been since she'd done that? Her life since she'd left Denver had been so filled with work—with setting goals and then achieving them. Finishing college and selling her first book had taken all her time and energy. It wasn't just that she hadn't ever ridden on a motorcycle before. She hadn't really taken any time for herself in years. Everything else had been too important.

Distracted by the scenery and the thrumming of the

bike beneath her, she didn't at first realize how tightly she'd wrapped herself around Nash. Probably because it had happened so gradually.

His body was different. It was impossible not to notice. As they crested a hill and shot down the other side, she found herself well and truly pressed against him. The muscles in his back were harder than she remembered, and his shoulders seemed wider. Or perhaps they only seemed that way because his hips were so lean and his waist so narrow and hard.

As they reached the bottom of the hill and their speed slowed, she knew she should draw back. But she badly wanted to get even closer.

He wasn't the boy she'd known. He'd matured into a man, but she was drawn to him just as surely as she'd been to the boy. She wanted to get to know Nash Fortune again. More than that, she simply wanted him. As if that simple acknowledgment was all her body was waiting for, she felt heat flood through her.

Suddenly, it was difficult to keep her hands where they were or to prevent herself from leaning her cheek against his back. It was even more difficult to keep her mind from wondering just what might happen if she pulled his shirt free and pressed her hands against his skin.

And she might have followed through on her desire if it hadn't occurred to her that eleven years ago, she'd never have even thought of taking the initiative in their love making. Nash had always taken on that role.

So she was different, too. What other differences would she discover if they made love again? The question was still lingering in her mind when Nash turned off the highway onto a narrow rutted road. Then she had to shift her whole focus to staying on the bike. She was aware that they were climbing higher, but trees pressed in on either side and the road grew rougher. By the time he finally pulled to a stop, Bianca couldn't feel her backside. Nor could she feel her legs as she climbed off the bike.

But as she stood next to Nash, she had to admit the view was worth it. Below them, the earth dropped away in a sheer cliff face to a silver snake of a river below them.

"Where are we?" she asked.

"It's a place my dad showed me before he went off to the Gulf War. He used to come here to think. He didn't say as much at the time, but I think he wanted to share it with me in case he didn't come back."

She turned to him then, but he continued to look down at the rush of water below them. "I'm sorry that you lost him."

"Me, too. But I'm glad he showed me this place. I haven't been here in years. Not since you left that note for me."

He met her eyes then, and she couldn't read the expression in his. Her stomach knotted and she felt the prick of tears behind her eyes. "I don't expect you to forgive me for that."

"It's not a matter of forgiveness. It's—"

"No." She raised a hand. "You deserve to know what happened. I need to tell you. Then you can decide. I haven't been able to think of much else since your grandmother contacted me about writing this book. But I need a promise first."

He raised his brows. "A promise?"

She nodded. "I know that I have no right to ask you for one. But I want one anyway. You have to promise that you won't blame anyone but me for what happened."

He tilted his head to the side and studied her for a moment. There was pain in her eyes. Years ago he would have given almost anything to know that she was suffering as much as he was. Now, he didn't like realizing that she must have. And if he was going to demand honesty from her, he felt obligated to step up to the plate.

"If you're referring to the fact that my grandmother bribed you to cut off our marriage plans and run away, Father Mike told me about that, and I confronted her about it years ago."

Bianca's mouth dropped open. Without thinking, Nash placed his finger under her chin to help her close it. It had been a mistake to let his gaze shift to her mouth. Her lips were unpainted, moist. And hadn't he been wondering about her taste ever since the night before when he'd taken her hands and brushed that kiss on her cheek?

All he'd have to do was take the smallest step closer and increase the pressure just a little on her chin, just enough to close the distance.

For just a moment, he let the idea of kissing her tempt him. His body grew even harder than it had on the ride up here. But based on his past experience with her, he could be pretty certain that he wouldn't be able to stop with just one taste. The chemistry they'd shared in the past had always been explosive, and neither one of them had shown much aptitude for controlling it.

If he went with his impulse now, they'd make love. If she was as responsive as she'd been when she was seventeen, it wouldn't take him long to convince her. In seconds, he could have her out of the neat shirt and slacks she was wearing, and those long legs would wrap around him as he entered her.

Then he would take her, they'd take each other right

here on the ground. For a moment, he let the temptation linger in his mind.

But that was the path they'd chosen eleven years ago. They'd been two teenagers who'd let their feelings and desires rule. Like greedy children they couldn't get enough of each other. Considering their history, it might be wiser to take a more cautious tack—especially until he had his strategy nailed down.

Reluctantly, he dropped his hand to his side just as Bianca took a step back.

"I… What did you just say?"

"You don't remember?"

"I will. Give me a minute."

The fact that she'd lost track of the conversation simply because he'd touched her was nearly enough to have Nash seriously reconsidering his idea of taking a more rational approach.

She met his eyes. "You knew all this time that your grandmother had bribed me?"

"Father Mike told me the night I found the letter. But I would have figured it out eventually. You couldn't have just disappeared like that without some help. And Grams was the prime suspect for something like that. When enough time had gone by, I even had to admire her style. When she wants something, she knows just what bait to put in the trap. And the kicker was that she and Father Mike both told me that if I loved you, I'd think of what was best for you before I did anything rash."

Bianca felt such a tightness around her heart that she nearly rubbed at it. "During those first few months, I was so sure you'd try to find me. I used to dream about seeing you again. The dreams always ended with you talking me out of my decision. Finally, I realized that you just hated me too much."

"I never hated you, Bianca."

"Not even after you learned I took a bribe? Your grandmother got me a scholarship to an Ivy League school, she got my Aunt Molly a wonderful job. In your place, I would have hated me. She even gave us start-up money to live on."

"I'd be lying if I said that I was happy with your decision. I was hurt, angry, and I was too pigheaded at first to see that I was being selfish."

"How were you selfish? I'm the one who took the money and ran away."

More than anything, Nash wanted to step forward, to take her into his arms and just hold her for a moment. But he didn't trust himself. "If we had married, I would still have graduated from the Air Force Academy and followed in my father's footsteps. But it's highly unlikely that you would have gotten to where you are today. I would have fulfilled my dream and you might have lost yours. Would you go back again and take that risk?"

For a moment, she thought about it. Then on a sigh, she shook her head. "No."

"Then it's a good thing I didn't come after you." He stepped forward then and took her hands in his, the same way he had at the party the night before. He felt her pulse jump beneath his fingers, felt his own leap to match it. "Would you have come with me if I had?"

"I don't know."

She had suffered, Nash thought. They both had. In the past.

"That was then and this is now, Bianca. I still want you. We can start over again with a clean slate."

She took a step back then, pulling her hands free. "I don't know if I want that. We're different people now. And I came here to work. Not to start over again with you. I can't, I won't jump into something again. We could end up hurting each other again."

That was the risk, Nash thought. Hadn't he already decided that he was going to take it? His impulse was to reach for her hands again. But he needed a different strategy for convincing her than he'd used the last time. Perhaps this time they needed to do it her way. No jumping. Yet.

"We don't have to decide today. We'll go slowly this time. For the time being, while we get to know each other again, we'll keep our relationship strictly professional. Fair enough?"

She said nothing for a moment, as if she was looking for the pitfalls in his offer. And they were there. He was planning on them. Patience might not be his long suit. But he could muster some up when he wanted something badly enough.

He smiled at her. "C'mon, Bianca. It's my best offer. And we do need to work together."

She nodded then. "Okay. For now."

"Then we have a deal." But he didn't offer her a handshake. Instead, he said, "Believe it or not, I didn't bring you out here to talk about us." And somehow on the ride up here, he'd completely lost track of his true purpose. "You haven't lost your ability to sidetrack me completely." Or to make him want to simply sweep her away.

"It's a mutual problem," Bianca said. "I intended to tell you about the bribe even if you refused to see me again. But that's not the main thing I wanted to talk to you about, either."

"I know." Nash gestured her toward a long flat rock and sat down on one facing her. "You came to my office—in fact, I suspect you took the writing job that my grandmother offered you—because you're looking into the disappearance of Brian Silko."

When she opened her mouth and then shut it, he said, "Hold that thought." He rose, walked to a compartment on the back of his motorcycle, and pulled out a small basket. "We'll discuss it over lunch."

5

By the time Nash had spread out the contents of a small wicker basket onto a snowy white tablecloth, the "lunch" would have made a good photo op for a glossy gourmet magazine.

While he poured red wine into two plastic glasses, Bianca continued to study the small meal. It was easier to concentrate on that than it was to look at him. Or to think about clean slates.

The fact that they'd agreed to keep their relationship professional for now didn't alleviate the fact that everything about him still tugged at her senses. Nor could it change the fact that there was a part of her that didn't want to be professional at all.

Yaaay!

Bianca firmly ignored her inner voice, but she wasn't as successful in ignoring Nash. He was dressed in full uniform minus his jacket. The shirt was short-sleeved, and despite averting her eyes from him, she'd gotten more than one look at his muscled forearms as he'd unpacked the food.

The array he'd spread out on the rock was sparse but elegant—some crackers, dried salami and something in a tin that she suspected was caviar. On a similar picnic years ago, he'd introduced her to the taste. But it had taken her a while to cultivate it.

When he handed her a wineglass, she met his eyes over the rim. "You planned this."

"Absolutely not. I knew that I wanted to talk to you in a more private venue, but it wasn't until I stepped into the hallway and saw you that I thought of this spot. So I went with it."

His story sounded very much like the Nash she remembered—impulsive, romantic. A bit on the wild side. The appeal of that, of him, hadn't waned. But right now she wasn't going to think about that or the clean slate he'd offered. That was for later when she wasn't alone with him in the middle of a very private wilderness.

She shifted her gaze back to the food. "Do you always carry a spare picnic around with you?"

"As a matter of fact, I do."

She heard the smile in his voice, but her eyes didn't stray from the salami. Okay, perhaps they strayed to his hands as he deftly sliced the meat. She remembered how she'd felt the pressure of each one of his fingers when he'd gripped her wrists at Maggie's party and how her pulse had throbbed.

"I replenish my supplies regularly. Red wine doesn't need chilling. When I ride the bike, I sometimes end up in isolated places, and I like to be prepared. Military training, I suppose."

She said nothing. When he offered her a slice of salami on a cracker, she shook her head, knowing that if there was any contact between them, even a casual brush of her fingers against his, she might tremble.

"Bianca, darling, if I'd *planned* on bringing you here, I'd have chilled some champagne."

And he would have, she thought. That had been the Nash she'd known and fallen helplessly in love with. The first time they'd made love, he'd brought champagne. Somehow, remembering that eased some of her tension. She lifted her glass and sipped the wine. "Why *did* you bring me here?"

Before answering, he spread caviar on a cracker and set it on a napkin in front of her. "I wanted a place where I could get the answers to my questions in private."

Bianca's eyes narrowed. "Your office isn't private enough?"

"General Winslow dropped by to see me shortly before you arrived. He warned me that you were the kind of person who dug up secrets and he asked me to pass along the official Air Force Academy's position on the disappearance of Brian Silko—which is no comment."

Excitement shot through her. "Then there *are* secrets."

"That was my thought, too," Nash said. "That's why you're really here in Denver, right? To find out what happened to Silko?"

She met his eyes steadily. "I'm here to investigate two stories—Brian Silko's disappearance and the early history of your family, specifically the disappearance of Jeremiah Fortune shortly after he and your great-great-great-grandfather discovered gold."

"According to the oral tradition, the two brothers fought over a woman, Thaddeus won, and Jeremiah was hung two years later for stealing a horse."

"Those are the broad strokes. Maggie wants me to fill in the details and then to continue on down to the present day." She gestured toward him with her glass. "To you."

He picked up his own wineglass and sipped. "How do you start investigating something like that?"

"Your grandmother says there are piles of stuff in the attic. Fortunes never throw anything out. I'll start this afternoon, and if I can find a thread, I'll start pulling at it and see where it leads."

He studied her for a moment. "You're really interested in writing about the Fortunes, aren't you?"

"I have been ever since your grandmother approached me about the job. I have a feeling about it—the same feeling I have about the Silko story. There's something there."

"I hope you find it." He spread caviar on a cracker. "Grams went to a lot of trouble to get our paths to cross again."

"I realize that. But why?" She had to inch forward on the rock to take the cracker Nash offered and she bit into it.

"She wants someone to run Fortune Enterprises. I think she's hoping for grandchildren. In the short term, I think she wants us to get back together."

Bianca's eyes widened. If she hadn't swallowed the cracker, she might have choked on it. "You're kidding."

"No. The one thing you can take to the bank about Maggie Fortune is she plans ahead."

"But you can't... She can't... I don't..."

He placed a hand on the side of her face. She felt the pressure of each one of his fingers. "There's no need to panic."

But it wasn't panic she was feeling now. They were face to face. Eye to eye. Close enough that she could see the darker flecks in those sky blue eyes. Those fascinating eyes.

"All she's giving us is an opportunity to get re-acquainted."

It occurred to Bianca that she should get up, move away. He might let her, and he might not. Which did she want?

How was she supposed to think it through when his mouth was so close that she could feel his breath on her lips? For an instant everything narrowed to one sharp desire—she wanted his mouth on hers. His lips were so firm…and his taste, would it be the same as she'd remembered? Or would that, too, have changed?

Go ahead. Find out. You know you want to.

For once, she had no argument with that little voice inside of her. All she had to do was close that tiny distance that remained between them. Then she would know.

But taking that taste would be so dangerous. And kissing Nash wasn't what she'd come back to Denver to do. Not even one of Maggie Fortune's elaborate plots could make her do it. But there was such a yearning that was building inside of her. Should she? Shouldn't she?

While she teetered on the brink, Nash dropped his hands from her face and inched back a little.

Close call, he thought to himself. Another second or two and he'd have become very unprofessional. He'd have kissed her. And more. He still could. Those green eyes of hers were still dark and clouded. A pulse was beating frantically at her throat. He wanted his mouth right there so he could feel her desire, taste it. No other woman had ever made him feel this way. Ache this way.

And it wasn't just the memories that were tempting him, though they accounted for some of the pull. He had no doubt at all the desire twisting painfully inside of him was for the woman sitting in front of him.

He'd told her they would go slowly, but it was nearly killing him to keep his word. His palms were literally itching with the need to touch her. He reached for his glass of wine instead. And his hand trembled.

No one, nothing had ever had that effect on him. He lifted the glass slowly and took a swallow. "Now that we've speculated about my grandmother's desires, maybe we should talk about what we want."

"I want to discover Brian's and Jeremiah's stories."

"Okay. I have to admit that both of your projects have piqued my interest, too. I also want you, and you want me."

She wrapped her arms around herself. "I need to think about that. And you said we'd go slowly."

"Then I need to think about something else right now."

"Right."

He was pleased to find that when he reached for the wine bottle, his hand didn't tremble. He topped off both of their glasses. "Let's try this. Brian Silko. I assume you want to know what I remember about him."

"I do. You knew him."

Nash put the cork back in the bottle and began to repack the picnic basket. "Not well. I thought about it after General Winslow left my office earlier. We were on the football team together, but he was a kicker. We were never on the field at the same time. And he didn't hang out in the locker room very much. The only private conversation I can recall having with him was one weekend when I happened to give him a ride into Denver. All we talked about was flying. He loved it."

"Didn't your fellow players on the football team have

theories when he disappeared? There must have been gossip."

"Sure they talked about it. Some believed that there had to be a girl at the bottom of it. And he had a rep for being an excellent pilot. There was some gossip that he 'borrowed' a plane to take a joy ride and it ended in tragedy."

She frowned a little. "But the police never discovered any girlfriend and his instructors claimed he was a serious, straight-A student, not the type to steal a plane on a lark."

When he raised his brows, she said, "I've been in Denver for two days, and your grandmother very kindly pulled a few strings so that I could look at the old police files. From what I read, the Colorado Springs police worked hard on the case, but they simply couldn't find anything."

She'd done her homework, but he wouldn't have expected any less. It occurred to Nash that he'd made a decision. In spite of the fact that General Winslow had made it clear that the Air Force Academy didn't want Bianca stirring up the old story, he was going to help her if he could. Because his grandmother was right and he was bored? Because he was curious? Because it would give him an excuse to stay in professional contact with Bianca?

All of the above. He bit back a grin as he closed the picnic basket. Then he met her eyes. "What got you interested in this particular case?"

"Anonymous notes. Two months ago, I discovered the first one at a book signing. A young woman had tucked it under a pile of my books. All I caught was a quick glimpse of her, but I'm pretty sure I signed a book for her. I can't remember her name, but it made me remember the incident. My editor got the second one. She did a quick Google search and encouraged me to poke around some more. The third one came in the mail, and it said that Brian Silko wasn't dead and that the secret lay somewhere at the Air Force Academy."

"That's pretty cryptic," Nash said.

"Yes, but what if he *is* alive? My editor's note was postmarked from Denver, and the one I received was stamped from the Air Force Academy."

"Do you still have them?"

She nodded. "They're in my car."

"I'd like to see them and have Gabe Wilder take a look at them. His security firm is the best. Jonah may have some ideas, too. On the surface, he's turned into a legitimate businessman, but he has exceptional computer skills."

"Are you sure you want to help me? General Winslow won't be pleased."

Nash grinned. "All the more reason to enlist Gabe and Jonah. That way I can keep a low profile."

Her brows shot up. "Riding away with me on your motorcycle doesn't seem to fit into the low-profile category."

He shrugged. "Let me worry about the general. I'm becoming very curious about what happened to Brian Silko." He reached over and put a finger beneath her chin. "There will be consequences, Bianca. If we work together on this, we're going to make love again. I can give you some time to think, but I know what we're both going to be thinking about. We're not going to be able to ignore what's between us and what there might be for very long."

"We're adults now," she pointed out. "We have more control than we had as teenagers."

He smiled at her. "I agree." Then he rose, tucked the wicker basket beneath one arm and reached for her hand with the other. "That's part of the allure, don't you think?"

6

THE RINGING OF THE PHONE had Bianca sitting straight up in bed and grabbing the receiver. Her hotel room was pitch dark except for the glow of the digital clock radio on her night stand. 2:00 a.m.

"Hello?"

"Ms. Quinn."

The deep, rough-edged voice didn't belong to Nash. Disappointment stabbed first, then puzzlement. "Who—?"

"Remember what curiosity did to the cat. Forget about Brian Silko."

A chill raced up her spine. "Who is this?"

The only response was a dial tone. She stared at the receiver for a moment. She could call Nash. Why? To tell him what? That she'd received a phone call in the middle of the night warning her off the Brian Silko story?

Annoyance pushed against the fear as her mind cleared. The phone call wasn't Nash's problem. Or it shouldn't be. And whether or not to call him wasn't the question. The question was, who had called her and what did it mean?

General Winslow clearly didn't want her poking into the disappearance of an Air Force Academy cadet. But an anonymous, mildly threatening phone call in the middle of the night didn't seem the Air Force's style.

Still, who else had voiced an objection to her looking into the story?

Pressing her hands against her temples, Bianca lay back down on her pillow. One thing was certain. She'd rattled someone's cage. That was the good news.

The bad news was that her first impulse had been to call Nash. And she wasn't sure that her motivation had been only because the phone call had initially frightened her. He'd said that neither one of them would be able to stop thinking about what they might have together. And he was right.

Then there was the problem of General Winslow. If he was the one behind the phone call and he found out that Nash was helping her, it could very possibly impact Nash's career in a negative way.

Those were the problems that kept her staring at the dark ceiling of her hotel room a long time before she fell back asleep.

It must have been the tenth box she'd opened that day, but Bianca felt something the instant she pried off the lid—a sense of nervous anticipation. When she saw the yellowed newspaper, the feeling shot straight to her gut. Then she sneezed. Dust flew. Turning her head, she sneezed again, this time stirring up even more dust a few feet away. She held her breath waiting for everything to settle again.

The attic of the Fortune Mansion hadn't been cleaned in years. Perhaps half a century or more. But what would have been the purpose? There was nothing here but piles and piles of boxes, cartons and crates. Maggie had been right. The Fortunes never threw anything out. Holding her breath, she carefully pulled the box along the floor and out of the dark corner where she'd found it.

Yesterday afternoon when Grady had first shown her the attic, she'd actually gasped out loud, and the look the old family retainer had given her had held sympathy. "Sometime during the 1920s, Ms. Fortune's father-in-law hired someone to label the boxes that were here then. They should help."

They had. By the end of the first afternoon, she'd discovered that information on the older generations took up space near the walls, and various-size heaps advancing like the spokes of a wheel toward the center offered information on the later Fortunes.

The attic space itself wasn't enormous—probably some forty by forty feet, but the ceiling was high and criss-crossed by rafters. Two air conditioners had been placed in windows to wage a losing battle against the buildup of heat. When she'd finally dragged her box to a spot where the sunlight poured through the gabled windows, she stopped and sank to her knees beside it.

Yesterday afternoon, she'd found the work hot, dirty and totally fascinating. She'd gone home with a hopelessly soiled pair of linen slacks and the family Bible Maggie had asked Grady to give her. Studying the family tree had been fairly simple. Thaddeus I had only had one son and heir and the next four Thaddeuses including Maggie's husband and son had only produced one son and heir. Nash would have been Thaddeus VI if Maggie hadn't insisted his middle name be Nash after her side of the family.

With a sigh, Bianca sat back on her heels. In spite of all her efforts, she was thinking of Nash again. Just as she'd thought about him throughout the night. And she still hadn't decided what to do. Of course, she had to tell him about the phone call. Just as she had to at least offer him the option of not working with her on the Silko case.

But there's a part of you that wants him to work with you on that—and your motivation is not all case-related. That's why you haven't called him. That's why you're up here in this attic for the second day.

Since she figured her inner voice was right on the money for most of it, she firmly turned her attention back to the box. As she carefully lifted the yellowed newspapers, she felt that tingle again. Two copies of the *Indian Springs Gazette,* dating back to 1862. July.

The pages were fragile, so she turned them carefully. On the last page of the first one, she found the name she was hoping to find. Jeremiah Fortune. The story was short. There'd been a fight at the Golden Chance Saloon where the owner had accused Jeremiah of stealing a horse. Jeremiah had been taken to jail.

Setting the first paper aside, she opened the second one. Her stomach clenched when she found Jeremiah's death notice on the last page. He'd been found hanging from a tree near his house. So the broad-stroked story that had been passed down orally was right on that detail. She ran her finger slowly down the short column as she continued to read. No mention of how the hanging had occurred or how he'd gotten from the jail to his house. But her pulse jumped when she read the last line. Jeremiah was survived by his wife. No name was given.

Bianca spent the next hour rereading both of the newspapers again. There was no other mention of Jeremiah Fortune or his wife. But she had some clues—the wife and the name of the city he'd died in.

She was about to set the newspapers back in the box, when she spotted it—a leather bound book in the bottom of the box. Her cell phone rang just as she placed it carefully on her lap.

Nash, she thought as he put it to her ear. "Hello?"

"Bianca, this is Nicola Guthrie. Do you remember me from Maggie Fortune's party?"

"Of course." Bianca instantly recalled the pretty woman who was engaged to Gabe Wilder. "I never forget a fan. How are you?"

"Fine. I meant to call yesterday, but things got away from me at the office. I was wondering if you were free tonight?"

Bianca flicked her gaze over the cartons she'd yet to tackle. "I could be."

"Father Mike mentioned you play poker, and he can't make it to Gabe's monthly game tonight. We could use another player, and I could definitely use female company."

"I'd love to." The words were out before she could prevent them. Her Aunt Molly had started teaching her five card stud when she was a child, and up until her aunt's death, Molly Quinn had hosted a monthly poker game at her house.

That isn't the only reason you jumped at Nicola's invitation. You're hoping Nash might be there.

"Great." Nicola gave her the directions to Gabe's apartment. "See you at seven."

Bianca frowned at the cell phone before she tucked it back into her jeans pocket. So what if she was hoping Nash was there? She could tell him about what she'd discovered about Jeremiah. And the phone call.

Those are not the only reasons you want to see him.

Her stomach growled. Surprised, she glanced at her watch and saw what the complaint was about. It was nearly 1:30 p.m. That made it just about twenty-four hours since she'd seen or heard from Nash.

Look who's counting.

She pressed her fingers against her temples and closed her eyes. It was ridiculous. She hadn't seen or heard from the man in eleven years, and now he was dominating her thoughts again. She'd wanted to call him in the middle of the night. She wanted to call him now.

Which meant that she wasn't going to. Determined, she pushed him out of her mind and focused on the leather bound volume she'd found in the bottom of the box. The book looked to be homemade. The cover was soft. Opening it, she found a small leather pouch. Inside was a pendant with turquoise stones set in a spider's web of intricately woven silver.

Bianca held it up to the light. The design was eye catching. She'd never seen anything like it before. The pendant hung from a soft leather cord. Unable to resist, she looped it around her neck and then turned her attention back to the book. But the pages were blank. The only other thing she found tucked into the center of the book was a photo.

The tingling feeling sizzled through her again. Two men stood with the hills behind them, and in between stood a tall, willowy brunette. The picture was grainy, and it had been taken from a distance, but one of the men looked a lot like the oil portrait of the first Thaddeus that hung in Maggie Fortune's office.

The other man must be Jeremiah. Could the woman standing between them be the one who split the brothers up?

There had to be more. After carefully setting the items aside, she moved back down the aisle and started opening new boxes.

WHEN NASH ENTERED the attic, he found her sitting cross-legged in front of a crumbling box, poring over something that looked like a picture album. Sunlight, thick with dust motes, streamed in from one of the gabled windows and haloed her hair. For a moment, he forgot why he'd broken the speed limits getting here, and he simply experienced the sensation of years falling away.

She wore her blonde hair pulled back in a ponytail, much as she had when she'd been seventeen. The clothes—jeans and a T-shirt—were hauntingly familiar, too. So was the frown of concentration on her face. How many times had he come upon her in Father Mike's office proofreading the newsletter she'd put out for the St. Francis Center?

He knew that if he moved closer, he'd find that her scent was the same also, some thing that had always reminded him of spring flowers.

In the twenty-four hours that he'd managed to stay away, she'd slipped into his thoughts at the oddest times. This morning his mind had wandered right in the middle of a class. He'd been halfway through drawing a strategic flight plan on the board when he'd completely lost his train of thought. It had taken one of his students clearing his throat to bring him back. Even then, he'd stared blankly at the board for a moment.

He'd told himself that he was keeping his distance from her because he'd promised to give her time to think. But he'd also been testing himself. He'd kept track of her whereabouts by calling Grady, and he knew that she was working at the Fortune Mansion.

Grady had offered to give him her cell phone number, but he'd resisted the urge to take it. One full day—that's how long he'd promised himself that he'd go without contacting her. And he'd kept his promise—barely. As it was, he'd left the academy the instant his office hours were over. It hadn't been until he'd hit traffic at the outskirts of Denver that he'd recalled following the same kind of routine eleven years ago.

That year—his second semester in college—it had all been about getting to Bianca and stealing what time they could to be together.

Right now, he was battling the impulse to go to her, take the dusty book out of her hands and pull her into his arms. But she'd been right about one thing. The stakes were much different now. Higher.

Thirty offered a different perspective than nineteen. And he owed her the time he hadn't given her when they were younger. Perhaps he owed them both that time. Cautiously, he put his hands in his pockets and remained where he was. "Interesting reading?"

Startled, she dropped the album. "I didn't hear you." But she'd been thinking of him. It was the third or fourth time the photos had blurred on the page and her thoughts had drifted to him. Perhaps because she'd discovered what looked to be a love story in the album—Thaddeus Fortune and his wife Clementine's first years together. There was only one thing nagging at her.

"You were miles away." Nash glanced around. "I hope my grandmother's paying you enough to sort through all this."

"It's fascinating work. And I think I may have found something." She carefully closed the album she'd been reading and got to her feet. First she told him what she'd found in the old newspapers. Then she showed him the pendant and the photo she'd found in the handmade book.

Nash studied the photo. "So you think this is the woman responsible for splitting up my ancestors."

"That was my initial thought. But I'm not sure."

Nash met her eyes and saw the glimmer of excitement. "What?"

She placed the album on a chest and opened it. "These are pictures of Thaddeus and his wife Clementine."

Nash studied the photos as she flipped the pages. Clementine was a pretty blonde about medium height. The wedding photos on the first page segued into a pictorial story of the first years of Thaddeus's marriage, including baby pictures of Thaddeus II.

He glanced up and met Bianca's eyes. "She's not the woman standing between Thaddeus and Jeremiah in the other photo."

"No, she's not. And Jeremiah left a wife behind when he died. If the brothers had a falling out over a woman, maybe the brunette's the one and not Clementine. And maybe Jeremiah ran off with her."

"So you're thinking Thaddeus got the gold mine and Jeremiah got the girl," Nash mused.

"If that's how it went down." She lifted the pendant at her neck. "And then there's this. What was it doing in a pouch tucked into a book that held nothing else besides the photo?"

"Good question," Nash said. "Looks like you've got the threads you were looking for."

"I'm going to try to find out what happened to the brunette. I have a feeling that there's more of a story here than anyone might have anticipated. Let's hope that Indian Springs has records that go back that far. I thought I'd wear the pendant for a bit of good luck."

"I might be able to enhance your luck even further. Why don't I give Gabe the photo and see what technological tricks he might have up his sleeve to enhance it? And he may have some ideas on how to access the information you need in Indian Springs."

"I can talk to him. I know you're busy with your classes."

"Not too busy." He smiled at her. "I promised Grams I'd help you with the Fortune saga."

Bianca drew in a deep breath. "But *I* asked you to work on the Silko case. And I'm having second thoughts about that."

The flash of anger he felt surprised him. So did the hurt. Both were so reminiscent of the feelings that had swamped him in that long ago moment in the prayer garden that he didn't say anything for a moment. An attack of cold feet, that's what she was having. He could understand that. His own were a little chilly. Wasn't that the real reason he hadn't called her?

Leaning in, he tortured himself by brushing his mouth across hers. But he didn't linger. That wasn't the answer any more than anger was. His strategic plan to go slowly with Bianca included neither. So he smiled easily and said, "Nice try. But we also agreed to work together on that story. I'm not going to let you change your mind this time, Bianca. Unless you're a coward…"

Her chin lifted immediately. "I'm not. It's not that I'm changing my mind. But I got to thinking last night that I don't want to jeopardize your career in the Air Force. General Winslow—"

"I'll handle the general."

"I got a phone call last night. I couldn't recognize the

voice." She told him the message. "The general leapt to my mind as a prime suspect."

His eyes narrowed on hers. "That doesn't sound like General Winslow. But that's one of the reasons you want to step back and work on the Silko case on your own. To protect me."

"Yes."

"Well, while I appreciate the fact that you want to take care of me, that's not the way it works in the Air Force. We take care of one another. And we don't go off on our own. Or hold back information. From now on, you're my wingman, and I'm yours when it comes to the Silko investigation. You get any more threatening phone calls, you tell me right away. Agreed?"

"Yes. Okay."

"But that's not the only reason you're having second thoughts about us working together, is it?"

She said nothing.

"You could try telling me you don't want me. See if that works."

It wouldn't. He had to feel her pulse racing beneath his fingers. She certainly did.

"I didn't know that you'd interfere with my concentration."

His smile widened. "I'd say that we're in the same boat there. When I dropped you off at your car after our impromptu picnic, I promised myself that I wouldn't contact you for at least twenty-four hours."

She stared at him. "Really?"

"It was a near thing. I was very tempted to cancel my class this morning, not to mention my office hours this afternoon. So you're interfering with my work also."

"What are we going to do?"

"That's not something you should ask me when we're alone in an attic together."

For a moment silence hummed between them, and neither of them moved.

"Do you remember when we made love in the storage closet at the center?" Nash asked.

The memory had flickered to life even before he mentioned it. The first time they'd made love, he'd taken the time and the care to seduce her. Flowers and champagne. But that night in the storage room had been all heat and desperation. Glorious. The secrecy and the threat of discovery had added even more of a thrill.

"I'd never done anything like that before." Her voice sounded a bit breathless. The circumstances had been very similar to what they were right now. They'd come across each other by accident. She'd worked late at the center, and he'd come there out of habit—to use the basketball court just to work off some steam. They hadn't expected to run into each other. They certainly hadn't expected that lust would drive them into a storage room.

He'd smelled the same that evening as he did now—a mix of sweat and sun and something that was very male. Her gaze dropped to his neck. The shirt collar lay open, and his skin was damp just as it had been that night. Her throat went dry as dust. For a moment she let herself think of what might happen if she gave into the temptation to taste him right there.

She might have given in to it. She certainly wanted to. She might even have been leaning forward when she saw the thin chain. It hung around his neck until it disappeared beneath his shirt. In the V of the open collar of his shirt, she saw the medal. St. Francis. The sight of it jarred her back to the present.

They weren't those two teenagers anymore, but she couldn't trust herself to have any more control than she'd had eleven years ago where Nash was concerned.

Fisting her hands, she pulled them free and took a careful step back, but she wouldn't allow herself to retreat farther. "I haven't thought everything through yet."

"Same goes here. But we're both wondering about what it might be like between us now."

"Yes."

She wasn't aware that her eyes had drifted to his mouth until she saw his lips curve.

"I think I might be able to demonstrate a little more finesse than I did that night in the storeroom," he said.

As her own lips twitched, she felt some of her tension ease. "At the time, finesse wasn't high on our list of priorities."

"No."

"We were so young and foolish. But we can't go back."

"Only forward. And I have a suggestion. I want to kiss you."

7

BIANCA'S SMILE FADED. "Kissing won't solve our problem."

He raised both hands. "Hear me out. Our…indecision about how to deal with our attraction for each other is interfering with our work. If we act on that attraction, we'll be worried about where it might lead us and intensely curious at the same time. Do you agree with my assessment?"

"Yes."

This time his smile was wry. "An extra problem for me is that once I'm curious about something, I can seldom resist finding out. At the same time, I've promised you and myself that this time we'll take things slowly."

He glanced around. "As attractive as the idea is, a quick roll around the attic doesn't quite fit the bill."

She ruthlessly ignored the little thrill that rippled through her system. "You're taking a long time to get to your suggestion."

He raised his hands, palms out, and smiled at her. "Just practicing the 'go slowly' thing. It's not my strength."

The gleam in his eyes reminded her of the truth of that. He'd always made the moves in their relationship. And she'd always followed. That had been part of the thrill. She angled her head, studied him. Was it the reason that she hadn't called him all day—because she'd been expecting him to take the lead again?

"I know you like plans. So I propose we take things one step at a time, starting with a kiss."

Suddenly, he was closer, and her heart gave a quick thud. Then he ran a finger tip over her bottom lip. "That way there'd be one less thing we'd be curious about. What do you say?"

Say? She had to get a breath first. Then she should say no. But as he ran his gaze over the path his finger had just taken, she said, "Just a kiss. No touching."

"Agreed."

"Hands behind our backs," she insisted. "And no cheating."

When they'd both put their hands behind their backs, Nash lowered his mouth. But he didn't kiss her. Instead, he caught her bottom lip between his teeth. The instant mix of arousal and heat flooding her system had her clenching her fists.

More. She was sure she hadn't said the word aloud, but she heard his sigh of satisfaction, felt his mouth cover hers. But there was no trace of the demand she'd expected. And none of the speed. He kept the kiss so soft, changing the angle again and again as if he had all the time in the world and was determined to take it.

Hunger built layer upon layer as pleasure saturated her system. His mouth was so warm. So patient. Why had she only remembered the heat? When he took the kiss deeper and his tongue finally tangled with hers, she was the one who stepped forward.

She managed to keep her hands behind her back, but she was shocked at how much she wanted them on him. She wanted to drag her fingers through his hair, to test the muscles beneath his shirt.

Nash knew he was sinking fast. Her lips were so soft, so pliant, her mouth so full of textures and flavors. He hadn't forgotten them, but the memories that had been haunting him for the past few days paled in comparison. And the desire that had been simmering in him since he'd spotted her from the terrace two days ago burst to life and spread through his veins like a flash fire.

Even as he clamped down on it hard, he had the answer to the question that had been on his mind for the last two days. Curiosity satisfied. Kissing her, lightly, teasingly, any way, was still different from kissing other women. *She* would always be different for him. Because she was the one. A sliver of fear shot up his spine.

Not enough to make him step away. Not yet. He wanted her with a desperation he'd never felt for any other woman. He ached to touch her, but if he did, he would be lost. He had to think. He had to maintain control if he wasn't going to take her right here.

But she was doing something to his mind that she shouldn't be able to do. She was filling it up until there was no one and nothing else but her.

This time fear stabbed, sharp enough to have him breaking off the kiss and taking a full step back. To his surprise, his knees were weak.

For seconds, there was nothing but a humming silence between them.

"Well, now we know," Bianca finally said.

"Yeah." And he had to get them out of the attic if he had any chance of keeping his word. "Why don't I take you out to an early dinner?"

Her eyes widened. "I can't. I just remembered. I have to shower and change. Nicola Guthrie invited me to a poker game at your friend Gabe's apartment."

Poker night. He'd totally forgotten it. How could that have happened? How could he have allowed it to happen? And he was staring at the answer.

He desperately needed a plan. Not the one he'd improvised on the spur of the moment to steal a kiss, but a real one.

"As it happens, I'm going to Gabe's, too. They're serious poker players. But they'll have food—some of the best take-out in Denver. How about I follow you to your hotel and while you're changing, I'll grab something to tide you over."

When she nodded her agreement, he was more than willing to lead the way out of the attic. He needed some air. Fast.

"I'LL SEE YOUR FIFTY, Jonah, and here's fifty more." Bianca pushed chips into the center of the table.

"I'll match that and raise you a hundred." Nash kept his eyes on Bianca as he tossed in two piles of his chips. Truth told, he hadn't been able to take his eyes off of her for most of the evening. His three kings warranted the bet, but he was more interested to see what she would do when it came her way again.

They were seated at a round table in the apartment Gabe kept over his offices at G.W. Securities, and the game had been going on for nearly three hours.

"I'm out," Gabe said.

His two friends were excellent poker players, each with their own style. Jonah was canny and shrewd, keeping his cards and thoughts close. Gabe intellectualized the game, figuring the odds and weighing his options as if he were casing a place to prevent a successful heist. Nash often suspected that both men were experts at counting cards and could, if they'd so desired, make a killing at a Las Vegas casino.

He preferred to bet on instinct, to gamble everything on a feeling. Or to fold a decent hand if instinct told him he'd lose. But tonight, his feelings had been clouded more than once by Bianca.

Next to him, Nicola frowned at her cards, but she added the required chips to the pile. Nash was betting she'd fold on the next round. Nicola was easy to read. Bianca wasn't.

She was a damn good poker player. The pile of chips in front of her had grown steadily throughout the evening. Her style wasn't flashy, and she'd folded as many hands as she'd played out. All the while the expression on her face remained as pleasantly cool as if she were at a garden party pouring tea.

She'd always had garden party hands, he thought as his gaze dropped to her fingers. He remembered how they'd felt on his skin years ago. But now that he'd experienced the sharp contrast between memory and reality, he wondered just how long he could wait to feel them on his skin again.

Out of the corner of his eye, he saw Jonah fold and ruthlessly refocused his attention on the cards.

"I'll see Nash's hundred and add one hundred more," Bianca said.

Nash shifted his gaze to her face, but it telegraphed nothing as she pushed chips into the center. He'd watched her for three hours and hadn't been able to find a pattern in her betting style. That surprised him. Fascinated him.

She'd won the largest pot of the evening by simply

matching Gabe's and Jonah's bets. Another time she'd bumped up the pot twice before she'd simply folded. Was that what she was doing now?

Bianca met Nash's eyes. He could read nothing in hers. "I'm in," he said, "and I'll raise you two hundred."

She didn't even blink. Admiration streamed through him.

Nicola gave a low whistle as she tossed her cards down. "Too rich for my blood."

Jonah leaned over to Gabe and said, "Side bet. I've got fifty that says she wins the hand."

"Do I look like a man who takes sucker bets?" Gabe asked.

Ignoring his friends, Nash grinned at Bianca. "Up to you."

She pushed the required number of chips into the center. "I'll call."

"You're not going to raise me?" Nash asked.

She smiled at him. "I'm curious to see what you bet that last two hundred on. What have you got?"

"Three kings." He spread his cards out.

"Nice, but there's no room for them in my full house." She laid two fives and three tens on the table. Then she pulled her winning chips in.

"Well played." Jonah smiled at Bianca.

"That's high praise from Jonah," Nicola said as she rose from the table. "I think it's time for some refreshments."

"Good call," Nash said. "Losing always makes me hungry."

Bianca eyed the tall stacks of chips in front of Nash. "You came out pretty well, I'd say."

"He usually does," Gabe said as he began to clear the poker chips and cards from the table.

"I'll help Nicola." Bianca rose and followed her hostess out to the kitchen area. It was tucked behind a granite counter at the far end of the room.

"Where did you learn to play killer poker?" Nicola asked.

"My aunt taught me when I was very young. She loved the game." And she hadn't played poker since her aunt's death. Tonight had been fun. Concentrating on the cards had also given her a break from thinking about Nash and the decision she was going to have to make.

"I'm having white wine, but I also have red." Nicola took a wine bottle and three beers out of the refrigerator.

"White wine sounds wonderful," Bianca said. "What can I do?"

"Just grab the tray of sandwiches out of the fridge. I picked everything up at a deli earlier. Gabe and I don't cook much. Our specialty is takeout."

"I'll be glad to transport the food," Jonah said and Bianca passed him the tray. He selected one of the sandwiches and took a bite before he carried the food away.

Nicola handed Bianca a glass. "I've been meaning to tell you that I love that necklace you're wearing."

With her free hand, Bianca touched the intricately woven silver pendant she'd found tucked in the blank book. "It's not mine. I found it in one of the boxes I'm going through at the Fortune Mansion. I'll have to give it back to Maggie, of course, but it seemed a shame for it to be hidden away. And I'm hoping it will give me luck with piecing together Jeremiah Fortune's story."

"You think it's connected?"

"I do. It's just a hunch, but I found it in a box that

contained newspapers documenting the death of Jeremiah."

Nicola moved in closer to study it. "The weaving of the silver is so intricate. It reminds me of some pieces that I saw a while ago in a high-end store here in Denver. The name escapes me. I'll ask my stepmother. She has a mind like a steel trap when it comes to jewelry." She sipped her wine. "I guess you never know what kind of secrets you'll discover once you start digging."

Gabe took the three beers Nicola had set on the counter, then turned to Bianca. "Nash brought the notes you received that spiked your interest in Brian Silko. While Jonah and I take a look at them, Nicola has a favor to ask you."

"Sure." When Bianca turned back to Nicola, she saw that the woman's cheeks were flushed.

"Sorry about that. I was going to try to be a bit more subtle." She shot Gabe's retreating back a rueful glance. "I must be driving Gabe nuts."

"About what?"

Nicola sipped her wine. "Wedding plans."

"Congratulations. When?"

"Not until February. Gabe and I decided to marry on Valentine's Day because it played such a big part in our getting together. Even though it's still over six months away, there are soooo many details to consider. I have a to-do list that goes on forever and it's only about one third the size of my stepmother Marcia's."

Bianca smiled. "I'm a list maker, too."

"I knew I liked you the minute I saw you at Mrs. Fortune's party."

Bianca realized that she'd felt the same way about Nicola. There were some people who elicited that kind of instant feeling of connection. That's the way it had been with Nash the moment she'd first laid eyes on him. Past Nicola's shoulder she watched him laugh at something Jonah was saying, and just the sound of it rippled through her.

Nash definitely wasn't a list maker. They were different in so many ways. It wasn't just that he was more impulsive than she was. She'd witnessed that several times just in the way he'd bet tonight. He was more romantic, too. While she'd showered and dressed at her hotel for the poker game, he'd made good on his promise to pick up something to tide her growling stomach over.

He'd brought her a chocolate milk shake from a fast food restaurant they'd frequented when they'd first been dating. Just thinking about it had her heart taking a little tumble. How much longer was she going to be able to avoid making the decision he was giving her time to make?

And she shouldn't be thinking about that now. She shouldn't be thinking of him at all. With an effort she turned her attention back to Nicola who was emptying chips into a bowl.

"What's the favor you'd like to ask me?"

"Maybe you're too busy," Nicola said. "I'll understand if you don't have the time."

Bianca put her hand on Nicola's arm. "I can make the time. What do you need?"

"You'll think I'm silly. But I'd like you to come with me to St. Francis Church. It's about an hour's drive up into the hills. It sits on the site of the old Franciscan Monastery that was built years ago, and it's been renovated. Father Mike says the masses on the weekends there, and he's going to marry Gabe and me."

She paused to sip her wine. "My stepmother is an amazing event planner. But we're having a difference of opinion on this one thing. And I don't want to turn into one of those raving Bridezillas you see on TV."

Bianca couldn't prevent the laugh. "Sorry. It's just very hard to picture you raving."

"Oh, I can. But I like to pick my battles with my stepmother. You have to be at the church to really see the issue. Is there any chance that you could come with me tomorrow morning?"

"I'd love to."

"If I pick you up at nine, we can be back to work here easily by noon. Will that work?"

"Perfectly."

When Nicola shifted her gaze to the men, Bianca followed suit. Jonah was using one of the computers in the office space at the far end of the room. Nash and Gabe were seated on the leather couches that were clustered in front of a huge flat-screen TV. On it, a baseball game was in progress but the sound had been muted. The two men had their attention focused on one of the anonymous notes she'd received.

As they read it, Jonah joined the other two, laying a sheaf of papers on the coffee table before selecting another sandwich from a nearly depleted tray. Gabe used a pair of tweezers to pass his note to Nash and pluck up another one.

Bianca found her eyes shifting to Nash's hands just as they had all too frequently during the poker game. Just watching as he tossed in chips or picked up his cards was enough to have her recalling the strength of those fingers on her wrists. The next time they kissed, there wouldn't be a no-touch rule in place. She shivered at the thought.

"Any more food out there?" Jonah called.

Nicola pulled another platter of sandwiches from the

fridge and Bianca grabbed another bowl of chips before they joined the men.

Nash had left space for her next to him. As she sat, he laid his arm across the back of the couch, and Gabe arranged the notes they'd been studying on the coffee table so that Nicola could see them. She took a hard look at them before she settled on the arm of Gabe's chair.

"What do you all think?" Bianca asked as she selected one of the sandwiches from the platter.

"Nash filled us in on how and to whom each of the notes was delivered." Gabe turned to Nicola and brought her up to date. "I'll have them tested for fingerprints, and we may get lucky with the one that was hand delivered to you at the book signing. Where was the signing?"

"Chicago."

"Nash says that you think you remember who left it. And she had you sign a book," Gabe said.

"I can't remember the name. But she was tall and slender with dark hair. Early twenties, I'd say."

"Could she have been part Native American?" Jonah asked.

All eyes shifted to him.

"Perhaps," Bianca said. "Why?"

"I just did some preliminary background work on Brian Silko. According to his application to the Air Force Academy, he was part Navaho."

Bianca frowned. "I didn't know that. We went to the same junior high and I interviewed him once before he moved to Phoenix."

"He was survived by his mother and a sister who was eight years his junior," Jonah continued. "Marianne Silko. She'd have been nine when he disappeared and twenty now."

"There was only a brief mention of his family in the

police report," Bianca said. "Just a notation that they'd been notified and questioned by the Phoenix police. There'd been no sign that he'd flown home in the plane and they claimed he hadn't contacted them. How did you find out all that?"

Nash patted her shoulder. "You don't want to know how Jonah finds things."

Nicola laughed. "I'm an FBI agent and *I* don't want to know. I might have to arrest him."

"Just pretend you're not here, Nicola," Jonah murmured. He turned to Nash as he reached for another sandwich. "I also have a list of the faculty and staff working at the Air Force Academy the year Silko disappeared. I cross-referenced it with the list of current faculty and staff. There are only two names circled—yours and Sergeant Daniel MacAuliffe's."

"Of course, Mac was there. He worked at the airfield," Nash said. "He took me up on my first parachute jump." He turned to Bianca. "I run into him fairly frequently. Why don't you come out to the academy tomorrow afternoon, and we'll pay him a visit."

"I can be there by one o'clock," Bianca said. Then she turned to Jonah. "You don't have current addresses for either the mother or the sister, do you? I had no luck trying to locate them in Phoenix."

Jonah grinned at her. "I have to leave something for Gabe's office to do."

"Ouch." Gabe sipped his beer. "I can get someone on that first thing in the morning."

Bianca met Gabe's eyes. "I wonder if there's another favor you can do for me." She pulled out the photo she'd found in the blank book. "Nash thought you might have some way of enhancing this so that we could get a clearer view of the three people. We're pretty sure one of them is Thaddeus Fortune."

Gabe looked at it. "I have someone who's pretty good at this kind of thing."

"Thanks." Then she swept her gaze around the group. "I don't know how to thank all of you. We're making progress. Whoever sent those notes is very anxious for someone to look into the disappearance of Brian Silko. And who would have more motivation than a younger sister. Not that I'm jumping to any conclusions yet."

"It's not a bad conclusion," Gabe said. "But one of the notes was postmarked from the Air Force Academy and another from Denver. Nothing from Phoenix."

"Perhaps this Marianne lives here in Denver now," Nash said. "Chicago is a direct flight from here—perhaps three or three and a half hours. First make direct contact at a signing, then send the notes to a writer who digs into cold cases. If it is the sister, then she might very well have remembered that Bianca went to junior high with her brother."

"But why all the secrecy and anonymous notes?" Nicola asked. "Why not just get in touch with Bianca directly?"

"Good question," Nash said. Then he shifted his gaze to his two friends. "I have another favor to ask. General Winslow has made it clear to both me and Bianca that he doesn't want anyone looking into the Silko disappearance." He told them what they knew and about the anonymous phone call Bianca had received during the night. "My question is, why is the general so worried about someone digging into this?"

"I can poke around a bit in his background," Gabe offered.

"I'd appreciate it," Nash said. "Sooner or later, he's going to get wind of the fact that I'm helping Bianca."

"Why don't we just ask him? We could always pay him a visit tomorrow after we track down Sgt. MacAuliffe," Bianca suggested as she rose to help Nicola gather up plates and empty glasses.

Jonah glanced at Nash. "A preemptive strike. That sounds like one of your strategies."

"Except that I'd like to keep a low profile for now," Nash said. "I'd like both of us to."

"I agree. I don't like the anonymous phone call," Gabe said. "You're going to have to keep a close eye on her. We don't know yet what kind of a hornet's nest the two of you are poking into."

Keeping an eye on Bianca was definitely on his agenda. The problem was that whenever his eyes were on her, he also wanted his hands on her. And he wasn't sure how much longer he was going to be able to stick to his promise not to rush her.

One thing he knew for sure. Life was a hell of a lot simpler when you were nineteen.

8

Bianca's hotel was located in the downtown area not far from Gabe's offices and apartment. The place catered to business travelers with its extended-stay suites and it provided a doorman as well as a good security system. Nash had checked it out when he'd been waiting for her to shower and change earlier in the day.

What he didn't like was the fact that his apartment was in Colorado Springs, more than an hour's drive away. And Gabe had been right on the money. They didn't yet know what kind of trouble they might stir up by looking into Brian Silko's disappearance. Twice on the short drive over, he'd found himself noticing headlights in his rearview mirror. One car had turned off six blocks ago and the other had gone straight when he'd made the turn for the hotel.

Jitters. He had them. And they just weren't about headlights. More than once during the drive over, his mind had returned to that kiss they'd shared in his grandmother's attic.

Hell, he was thinking about it right now. And also thinking about the fact that he was going to kiss her again before he let her shut the door of her suite on him.

The go slow plan wasn't going to keep him from having another taste of her.

And he bet that she was thinking about kissing him again, too. Climbing out of the driver's side, he circled and then opened her door. Neither of them had said a word on the short drive over. As they started toward the hotel's entrance, he locked the car with his remote.

"I'm not going to invite you up to my room," she said.

"Figured," he said.

"I'm not going to even let you escort me to my door. I've been thinking about it all the way over here and I think we should say our good-nights before I go into the hotel. You can watch me through the glass door until I get into the elevator."

"Sounds like a sensible plan."

"I like sensible plans. And I like sticking to them. I just haven't figured it all out yet." She stopped and turned to face him. "You've always been able to make me want to throw caution to the wind. But I'm not that kind of person. I don't think I ever was. If I had been, your grandmother wouldn't have been able to buy me off." She paused to draw in a breath.

Nash put his hands on her shoulders. "Who are you trying to convince—you or me?"

"Both of us. Me. I won't lie to you. There's a part of me that would like to be young and foolish and just let you sweep me away again."

He smiled at her. "That would be my pleasure."

She shook her head. "The stories—Brian's and now Jeremiah's. I want to discover them. They're important to me. I didn't expect that seeing you again would make me want you even more than I did before."

Nash's hands tightened on her shoulders. "Bianca,

you expect to say that to me and then I'm supposed to let you walk up to your room alone?"

She saw the heat in his eyes, and she knew what he was feeling. Everything inside of her was melting. If he hadn't been gripping her shoulders, she might have slid right to the ground. For one moment, she wanted nothing more than to give into what she wanted, what they both wanted. Words—they were her strength. She searched for the right ones. "I don't want to hurt you again."

"I don't want to hurt you, either. There are no guarantees, Bianca."

Somehow, he'd lifted her onto her toes, but he didn't pull her closer. "I'll let you go this time. But I need a kiss."

But he didn't just take it. The Nash she'd known so long ago would have. Instead, he was giving her the time to pull away, to just say "no." She felt her heart take another little tumble.

"It's perfectly safe."

Safe? Kissing Nash had never been safe.

"We're on a public street." He glanced up and down the block. "There are still a few pedestrians out. Your doorman is within sight. If we try to do more than kiss, someone will call the police."

It's just a kiss. You can be sensible when you get to your room.

Even as she lifted her arms and clasped her hands behind his head, she could see the word *mistake* in neon caps, blinking on and off in her mind. But she was the one who pulled his mouth closer. Because she needed to kiss him, too.

The instant their mouths fused together, his flavor poured into her like a drug. All thoughts of mistakes faded from her mind as heat shimmered through her until her blood boiled, her head spun, and the cement sidewalk shifted beneath her toes. She simply had no choice but to hold on to him.

This wasn't like the kiss they'd shared in the attic. This was different. This was new. Each sensation was so sharp, so clear. His teeth scraped against her bottom lip, and the shock of pleasure sparked another and another until there was nothing else. She was sinking fast into a world where the air was so thick she couldn't breathe. And she didn't care.

Nash felt as if he were about to go under for the last time. He'd given her a chance to stop him. To push him away. If she had, he might have been able to recover. Regroup. He might even have been able to drop his hands, step back and escort her to the doorman.

Maybe.

But she hadn't pushed him away. Instead, she'd wrapped her arms around him and pulled his mouth to hers. And the raw demand he'd tasted had sprung from her as well as him.

Heat speared up and spread with such ferocity that he pulled her more deeply into the doorway of a store and steadied both of them against a display window. In his mind, he saw the "no touch" rule burst into flames. Every curve and angle of her body was pressed against his, and his hands had already pulled her blouse free of her slacks.

When he took his hands on a quick thorough journey from her waist to the sides of her breasts, his muscle memory kicked in, and he drew her closer. There'd been other women since Bianca. But none had fit so perfectly against him. And he remembered just how perfectly she fit around him when he'd been inside of her.

He ran his hands back down to grip her hips and lifted her. She immediately scooted up, wrapped her legs around him. Pleasure stabbed at him so fiercely that his knees went weak. He pressed her back against the wall to keep his balance, and then he rocked into her.

When she made a helpless sound and arched in his arms, his need turned to a throbbing ache, and his hands moved automatically to the waist of her slacks. He'd opened the waistband before he registered what he was doing.

No one had ever pushed him to the edge like this. No one but Bianca. A sliver of fear worked its way up his spine, stilling his fingers. Some of the street noise surrounding them penetrated—the blast of a horn, the sound of music pouring out of a passing car's window. Nash suddenly remembered they were in a public place. Regaining his sanity, he dragged his mouth from hers.

"More." The word came out on a breath.

For a moment Nash wasn't sure if he'd said it or if the request had come from Bianca. He certainly couldn't disagree with the sentiment. He definitely wanted more. And he was outrageously tempted to take it. His fingers were still pressed against the soft damp skin below her waist, inches away from the slick core of her heat.

Her cheeks were flushed, her lips still moist and swollen from his. And in the dim light of the street lamps, he could see those witch green eyes were still clouded.

But even as he was tempted to move them both deeper into the shadows of the doorway and his fingers moved closer and closer to her heat, her eyes began to clear and she drew in a ragged breath.

"We have to stop," she said. "We nearly…"

"Yeah." He withdrew his hand and somehow managed

to press both his palms flat against the glass of the display window.

"I nearly..." Still holding on to him tightly, she slid her legs to the ground. "You nearly made me..."

"Yeah." And he still wanted to. He kept his hands against the wall. That much was vital. If he touched her again, he'd finish what they'd started.

"This is crazy," Bianca said as she fumbled with her slacks. "I knew that I shouldn't let you kiss me."

He didn't argue. All he'd managed so far was two "yeahs." Plus, she was right. Another moment and he would have taken her right there. Making love to a woman in a public place wasn't his usual style. It would have been a first, and there was a part of him that was already regretting the missed opportunity.

"I'm going to go up to my room and think this through."

Nash said nothing. If he'd wanted to persuade her that they should make love again, he figured he'd made his point. Dropping his hands, he stepped aside to allow her room to move away from the window.

He walked with her to the door of the hotel, but he was careful not to touch her as he delivered her to the smiling doorman. Remaining there on the street until the elevator doors closed behind her was one of the hardest things he'd ever done.

BIANCA MADE IT UP to her room. Barely. Once inside, she locked the door and leaned against it. She was still so aroused that she was sure if she pressed her legs together tightly enough, she might come.

And that wasn't the way she wanted to come. Resisting the temptation, she kicked off her shoes and then strode down the length of the room through the living area of the suite and into the bedroom. It wasn't until she reached the window that she stopped. When she climaxed, she wanted Nash to be inside of her—pushing in, pulling out.

But certainly not on a public street. She didn't even dare glance down. If she saw that doorway…just the thought had something deep inside of her tightening again. If they'd made love there, that would have been crazy. She'd have been crazy to allow it.

And you would have enjoyed every single second. If he'd slipped his finger into you, he'd have sent you soaring. You wouldn't have cared if you were in the middle of Times Square.

But even as she pushed that vivid image out of her mind, another one filled it—the two of them naked on her bed, their limbs entwined, every hard plane and angle of his body pressed against hers as they moved in unison together. She could almost feel the slick slide of their bodies against each other, the pressure of his penis filling her.

Thinking about it had that unbearable tension tightening inside of her again, and for a moment all she could do was lean her forehead against the cool glass of the window and take deep breaths.

But the image lingered, and that wasn't what she should be thinking about. Pushing the picture firmly out of her mind, she whirled around and sat down on the far side of the bed. Then she reached for the water bottle she'd left there earlier. When her hand gripped the receiver of the phone instead, she snatched it back as if it had given her an electric shock.

Was she going to call him?

That would be my guess. You memorized his cell phone number the instant Grady gave it to you. And

*when the elevator reached this floor, you immediately
reached for the button that would return the car to the
lobby.*

Raising her head, Bianca stared at her image in the
mirror that hung directly in front of her on the wall.
What had happened to her think-it-through plan?

*That doesn't seem to be going so well. Why not try
a new tack?*

Rising, she moved closer to the woman in the mirror.
"No. I'm not going to let Nash Fortune sweep me away
again. This time I'm going to have a plan."

*Why not borrow from the military? Define your ob-
jective, lay out the ground rules, and make sure you
have a reasonable exit strategy.*

Bianca frowned at her image as she thought it
through. "The objective is easy. I want to make love
with Nash."

*Then go for it. You're both adults. You're unattached.
You want each other. This should be a no-brainer.*

Her frown deepened. "But we hurt each other in the
past." Saying the words out loud made them sound even
lamer than when she thought them.

*You may hurt each other again. Life comes with risks.
And if you don't take them, you'll never know. If you
hadn't accepted Maggie Fortune's money and moved
east to college, you wouldn't be where you are today.
Thank heavens you weren't a coward back then.*

Bianca clamped her hands over her ears and turned
away from the mirror. "Enough with the lecture. I need
a minute here."

But the fact was her inner voice was making sense.
She and Nash were both unattached adults who wanted
each other. What was the big deal?

The ground rules could be simple. They would go into

their relationship this time with the full knowledge that it had to be temporary. She was only in Denver until she finished her work on the two books. They would enjoy each other until they had to go their separate ways.

Great. She had a plan. And she'd tell Nash first thing in the morning.

No. She pressed fingers against her temples. She'd promised Nicola to visit the church of St. Francis and Nash had a class. Later then—when she met him at the Air Force Academy. There would be time to lay out the ground rules for him before they talked to Sergeant MacAuliffe at the flight field.

There. She had a plan. It was settled. She turned and paced back to the mirror. "So why don't I feel settled?"

She raised a hand before her inner voice could answer. "Because I don't want to wait until tomorrow. I want Nash here in my bed right now."

Slowly, she smiled at the woman who stared back at her. "I'm going for it."

This time when she picked up the room phone, it didn't feel like an electric shock. Or maybe she just didn't notice that because her whole body seemed to be on fire as she pushed in Nash's number.

PATIENCE. THAT WAS going to have to be his mantra. But he still hadn't been able to start his car and pull away from the curb in front of Bianca's hotel.

He wasn't a patient man by nature. But it was a skill he'd had to hone during his military career. There was always a lot of downtime between missions. A lot of prep work to be completed before climbing into the cockpit.

Even getting his pilot's wings had taken more time

than he'd liked. Hell, he'd barely been able to wait until he'd graduated from the academy to begin his training as a pilot. He'd already had a civilian's license. But training to fly the fighter jets, that was something else. Extraordinary.

Of course, he'd been younger during his time at the academy and much more willing to throw caution to the winds, much *less* willing to think about the consequences.

That was the man he'd been when he'd first gotten involved with Bianca. Those were the excuses he had for the way he'd rushed her and pressured her into wedding plans. No one really looks very far into the future when they're nineteen. At that age, you're invincible.

But he wasn't now. And for the first time in any relationship with a woman, he was vulnerable. He liked women. He enjoyed their company, their views. He liked serving with them in the Air Force. He'd like to think that he was a kind and generous lover. But no other woman had ever mattered to him the way Bianca had. The way she still did.

That should be enough to have him being cautious. Wary. He shouldn't be having any trouble at all giving her the time she needed. But he was. There was no getting away from it. He wanted her with the same hormone-raging intensity he'd felt eleven years ago.

He glanced at his watch. Midnight. Nearly fifteen minutes had passed since he'd watched those elevator doors close behind her. He had no idea how long he'd stood in front of the glass doors of the hotel, but it had been long enough for the doorman to ask him if he needed directions somewhere.

He should go home. He had a class to teach in the

morning, and he'd see Bianca at 1:00 p.m. Instead, he was parked in a space outside her hotel room waiting.

For what? A glimpse of her at her window? He lifted his gaze to run it across the front of the hotel. Ridiculous. He didn't even know her room number. She probably didn't even have a view of the street.

Then he spotted her silhouette. She was backlit by the light from the room, but there was no mistaking the cloud of hair that fell to her shoulders or that slender-as-a-wand body. His heart literally took a little tumble. She was so close—only a matter of a few stories above him.

He found his fingers gripping the steering wheel. Was she thinking of him? Wishing that he'd stayed? Suddenly, he felt like Romeo standing in the Capulet garden waiting for a glimpse of Juliet.

Eleven years ago there might have been some excuse for his behavior. There was none now.

To hell with it, he thought as he drew out his phone. If he'd ever once hesitated this long when he was flying a mission, he'd have been dead or grounded long ago.

If he called her right now, there was a least a fifty-fifty chance she'd ask him to come up. If not, he'd just have to persuade her. He was about to punch in her number when his cell phone rang.

"I'm through thinking."

Nash was already climbing out of his car. "What's your room number?"

By the time she gave him the number, he was already striding across the hotel lobby.

9

BIANCA STARED DOWN at the receiver that she held in her hand. She'd actually called Nash and invited him up to her room.

So? Lightning is not going to strike you. You want him here. What's the problem?

She glanced at her image in the mirror. She could still call him back and tell him that she needed more time.

Coward.

Evidently not. She watched her hand set the receiver back into its cradle. It seemed to be operating of its own accord without any direct input from her brain. In fact, now that she'd made the call, her brain seemed to be operating in a kind of slow motion. She faced the mirror again. She should change.

Into what? It wasn't as though she'd planned this. She hadn't packed any sexy lingerie. She didn't *have* any sexy lingerie. If she'd just waited until tomorrow to call him, she would have had the time to…buy something.

She glanced at her watch. How much time had passed since she'd walked through her hotel door? Ten minutes? Fifteen? It would take him at least that long to drive back.

Rising from the side of the bed, she studied her reflection. She looked exactly as she had when she'd walked into the room. Her blouse was still pulled out, and beneath it, her slacks were still open—Nash had torn the button off. Her hair was tousled. In short, she looked as if she'd been ravished.

Well, only half-ravished.

She ran a hand through her hair. At least she could do something about that. Perhaps repair her make up. At least spray on some cologne?

Three staccato raps sounded on her door.

She didn't jump, but something deep and low within her did. She moved to the door, but not nearly fast enough. She felt as if she were pushing through water. She did remember to check the peephole, but once she'd seen Nash on the other side, she pulled the door open.

For a moment they just stood there, taking each other in. She already a vivid idea of what she looked like, her hair still mussed by his hands, her clothes just as he'd left them the last time he'd touched her, and her feet were bare. Still his gaze moved slowly from her face to her feet. Each time he lingered, that part of her body began to melt, and her toes curled into the carpet.

He looked about the same, too. The collar of his shirt was a bit rumpled, and his hair wasn't as neat as it had been in Gabe's apartment. Now that she was barefoot, he was a good foot taller than she was. And between his broad shoulders and his height, he completely filled her vision. And she wanted to eat him right up.

Meeting her eyes again, Nash said, "If you've changed your mind, this would be a good time to tell me."

"I haven't changed my mind."

A smile just curved his mouth. "Good."

Ditto. Though she could no longer feel her knees, she stepped back just far enough to let him enter the room.

He was the one who shut the door and latched it. But she made the first move by taking both his hands and stepping into his arms. The heat struck first as their bodies came into contact and melded, melted as if they were two parts of the same whole. She had a moment, just one, to savor the solid strength of him before she felt her breasts swell against his chest. She went light-headed with anticipation.

He slid his hands to her back, then down beneath her slacks to her bottom. His fingers might as well have been a brand. He gripped and lifted her so that she was pressed against the hard length of his erection.

"Wrap your legs around me again."

He hadn't finished the sentence before she did just that. He pressed her back against the wall of the room and rocked into her just as he had on the street earlier. It was as if no time had passed at all since he'd nearly slipped his finger into her. And this time there was no nearly. He slid his hand between them and moved it unerringly lower until his fingers probed and slipped into her heat.

"Nash." The word was half gasp, half whimper, and she wasn't sure if her intent was to stop him or to beg him to continue.

"I want you to come for me, now." He withdrew his fingers and probed again, this time deeper.

The climax shot through her in a series of ever-widening explosions. There was nothing that she could do but tighten her legs around him.

When her head stopped spinning, she realized that they were still just inside the doorway. The only sound was the sound of breaths going in and out.

Other details began to register. She was still wrapped around him, still pressed against the wall with her head tucked into his shoulder. His fingers weren't inside her anymore. But it wasn't his fingers she wanted inside her the next time.

She raised her head and met his eyes. "I do have a perfectly good bed."

"We'll get to it. But first, I wanted to finish what I started. I haven't been able to stop thinking of making you come since you walked out of my sight into those elevators."

"We haven't finished exactly. You haven't come yet."

"Yeah, I noticed."

What she noticed was that his penis was rock-hard and still pressed almost, but not quite, where she wanted it to be. Just thinking about having him inside her triggered another blast of heat that went straight to her toes. Instinctively, she inched herself up and tightened her legs around him.

"Bianca."

The rough-edged sound of the word sent a thrill through her and she would have arched against him if his hands hadn't gripped her waist and pressed her against the wall.

"Another move like that and you'll make me come."

She smiled slowly. "That's the idea. And you haven't even kissed me yet." In a quick move, she leaned in to bite his bottom lip.

The catch of his breath told her that he was totally under her power. She'd always known the effect he'd had on her, but she'd never before recognized that she might have the same effect on him. The realization was heady. Delightful. Irresistible.

"If I kiss you again, we won't make it to the bed," Nash said in the same low voice.

But he didn't move. His mouth was still there, hovering just a few millimeters away from hers. She could feel the heat of his breath on her lips and slipping between them. It would be so easy to just close the distance between them, to feel his mouth on hers again, but she wasn't quite ready to relinquish control. "We've never made love on a bed before."

They hadn't. She certainly couldn't have made love with him at her Aunt Molly's apartment, and Nash had never taken her to the Fortune Mansion.

"Good point." He maneuvered her through the small suite, and she was still wrapped around him when he put one of his knees on the foot of the bed.

"Clothes," he said as he disengaged her arms from around his neck and set her on the mattress.

The only light was from the small lamp on the desk. It washed over him as he pulled her blouse up and over her head. He grasped her elbows and drew her to her feet, then he slid his hands beneath the waistband of her slacks. For a moment, he gripped her buttocks again. The heat was so intense that she wanted nothing more than to climb up and simply melt into him again. But before she could move, he released her to push her slacks and panties to the ground. Her bra came next. In one swift move he'd unclasped it, and eased the straps down her arms until she felt the scrap of silk and lace drop to the floor.

It occurred to her that he was much more skilled at this than he'd been when he was younger. And a lot better than she was since she was now naked and he still wasn't. But when she reached for the buttons of his shirt, he caught her hands in his and held them out to the side.

Then he simply looked at her, letting his gaze linger first at her breasts and then lowering it slowly down the length of her body until each inch of her skin felt so scorched that she wondered blisters didn't form. All those muscles deep in her core began to quiver and tighten again. Was he trying to make her come again just by looking at her?

"Your clothes," she whispered. Pulling her hands free, she reached for his belt. With fumbling fingers, she managed to free it and the clasp on his slacks. Then he slipped one of his hard hands behind her back and caressed her breast with the other. His palms felt hot and hard against her bare skin, and when he rubbed his thumb over her nipple, the sensation swept away any thought she had of undressing him. All she knew was him and the way he could make her feel.

Then he was kissing her again with a thoroughness that sent every thought, every worry spinning away. He might be more skilled now, but his ability to spin her into a world where only the two of them existed was just the same.

At last, he joined her on the bed, and for one glorious moment his weight was crushing her. Her hips lifted, desperate for his thrust when he suddenly moved away.

"Nash." Her eyes flew open. He knelt beside her, still almost fully clothed as he sheathed himself in a condom. The thought drifted into her mind that he was definitely good at this. She hadn't once thought of safe sex. Not once.

Then he positioned himself between her legs. "Now."

"Right now."

Her eyes were open and on his when she felt him ease the head of his penis in. Then he paused. "Okay?"

"Not yet," she said. "I want all of you."

He pushed into her slowly, so slowly that she thought she might simply die of need before he was sheathed to the hilt. Then for a moment, they merely looked at each other, neither daring to move, neither wanting to.

She remembered those early times, his face, above hers, his eyes burning and midnight blue. The heavy press of his body against hers was both familiar and new. But all images and memories blurred into what was happening now. They might be different, but she felt the same connection with him that she'd felt from their very first time together. And she wanted more than anything to hold on to it.

Nash used every ounce of his control to stay still. He filled her. She surrounded him. And the fit was as perfect, as essential as it had been the very first time that they'd made love. Time spun out. He wanted it, too. Her face, the shadowy play of light across her features, the sea-green depths of those eyes—he'd carried this picture with him for eleven years without being conscious that it was there.

Once he moved, the need that sprinted fast inside of him—the ache to take her and make her his—would take over. And he needed a moment. He needed *this* moment. To savor. He'd made love to other women since Bianca, but no one had ever made him feel this way—as if he belonged right here.

But as much as he wanted to hold on to the feeling and on to her, his body made a small movement—a small stroke that triggered a stab of pleasure so sharp that it bordered on pain.

She gasped, her legs rising to grasp his hips. He felt her inner muscles tighten around him, milking him.

"All of you," she gasped. "Now."

He moved again, and he felt the first shudders, hers, his own, rip through him, and he was lost. They moved together now, in perfect rhythm as if they'd been born for it. She filled him, answering every need he'd ever imagined. Each time she dug her nails into him, each time she gasped his name, she urged him into a faster and faster pace, matching it until all reason shattered.

He was shooting through space, breaking all barriers. And all that mattered was that she was with him.

As REALITY TRICKLED BACK IN, Bianca registered that she was lying on the bed. One of her hands held Nash's, her fingers linked with his. The other was still clutched in his hair.

His body, as limp as hers was, lay sprawled over hers, his head nestled in the crook of her shoulder. His breath tickled the side of her neck as he breathed in and out.

He was heavy, but that didn't matter. Lying just this way in the dimly lit room seemed just right.

Perfect.

Well, not quite. Things hadn't gone exactly the way she'd planned. They hadn't agreed on the ground rules for their relationship. In fact the topic hadn't even come up.

At the moment, that didn't seem to matter, either. It was dangerous to be feeling this way, doubly dangerous not to be thinking up a new plan. But she couldn't seem to summon up the energy. There was so much pleasure just in feeling his body on hers, in listening to him breathe in and out.

Perfect.

"You okay?" His voice was a barely audible rumble.

"Mmm," she murmured.

She didn't even have the strength to protest when he raised his head and looked into her eyes. The concern she read in his had her sharpening her focus. "What's wrong?"

He raised his free hand to frame the side of her face. "It's been a long time since we've made love. I wanted to go slowly. You shot my plan to hell."

Delight was her first reaction. A ripple of power was her second. She smiled slowly at him. "Then we're even, I suppose."

"How so?"

"I wanted you naked."

"Really?" Grinning, he rolled over, pulling her with him. "We'll have to see if we can get it right this time."

"We can try."

His hand slid down to her bottom and for just a moment, she was tempted to just follow his lead. Then she levered herself up and shifted so that she was straddling his thighs. "Why don't I go first?"

Agreeably, he tucked his hands behind his head. "Go ahead. Take my clothes off."

The thrill that moved through her at his words was darker than the one he'd just given her with his hands. He'd lowered his pants, but his shirt was still almost fully buttoned.

She was about to reach for it, when out of the side of her eye, she spotted the condoms he'd dropped on the bedside table. On impulse, she reached for one of those instead. He kept his laser-blue gaze on her hands as she pulled off the old condom and sheathed him with the new one. While she worked, she felt him grow harder and harder beneath her touch. By the time she finished, she was so hot that she felt she might implode. And whatever plan she had of undressing him went out the window.

Instead, she lifted her hips and guided his penis into her heat. He rolled instantly, pinning her beneath him. "It's not going to be slow," he warned her as he began to thrust in and out.

"I guess you're not going to be naked." Then she locked arms and legs around him and matched his rhythm perfectly as they sent each other soaring again.

10

IT WAS NEARLY 5:00 a.m. when Nash climbed behind the wheel of his car. Leaving Bianca asleep in the bed was one of the hardest things he'd done in a long time. If he'd touched her again, he would have had to make love to her. He'd lost count of the number of times he'd reached for her during the night. His lips curved. Or the number of times she'd reached for him.

For just a second after he turned the key in the ignition, he hesitated and thought of going back up to her room. But he had an eight o'clock class and he needed a change of clothes.

Plus, if he knew women, and he did, after a night of lovemaking, they needed to talk. He didn't think that Bianca would be an exception. He pulled the car out of the space, made a U-turn and headed out of the city. Before they talked, he needed a plan.

Time he spent behind the wheel of his car or riding his bike was always good thinking time. And he couldn't seem to think at all when he was around Bianca.

She'd surprised him. He hadn't expected her to call him and invite him up to the room. Not that he was complaining. But he'd always been the aggressor in their relationship. She'd been a virgin when they'd first met. He hadn't. So it had been only natural that he'd take the lead.

And he'd wanted her desperately. From the minute he'd first set eyes on her, the chemistry between them had been something well out of the realm of his rather limited experience.

It still was. The difference now was that she'd seduced *him* last night. True, it hadn't taken much—three words over a cell phone. But it was as if she'd been the puppeteer and he the puppet. That was very different.

And she'd surprised him, delighted him with her lovemaking, too. She hadn't always been the seducer last night, but she'd done her fair share of it. And he'd been helpless to prevent it whenever she decided to take the reins.

Not that he had any complaints on that score, either.

But the one thing that hadn't changed about Bianca was that she was a planner. Even when they'd first met, she'd had her goal in focus. And, unlike him, she liked straight paths.

Turning his blinker on, he shifted his car into the right lane and took the entrance ramp.

One of the problems that had led to their break up was that he hadn't been on that path, and he'd convinced her to stray from it and elope with him.

Where was the fun in that? He liked the detours. He liked seeing where the next day and the next challenge led. When he'd been flying combat, he'd loved the excitement of seeing what challenges the next mission held. He thrived on having to decide on a dime what to do next.

But with Bianca, he definitely needed a plan. A better

one than his "go slowly" one which she'd shot to hell on more than one level. And he needed a better one than he'd had at nineteen.

Because he was not going to let history repeat itself. This time, he wasn't going to let Bianca slip out of his life.

"THANK YOU SO MUCH for coming with me," Nicola said as she unlocked the front door of the old church building.

"My pleasure," Bianca said as they stepped into the small vestibule. It had been a pleasure to have a distraction. On the drive up, Nicola had given her a brief history of the small church. It had been preserved and renovated when the rest of the original Franciscan Monastery that had once stood on the site had been torn down. Father Mike, now in semi-retirement, said three masses there every Sunday.

The easy conversation with Nicola as well as the breathtaking scenery of the drive had kept Bianca from worrying about her impulsive decision to invite Nash into her room last night.

Not that she regretted it. If it had been a mistake she was more than willing to pay the price for it—eventually. But she hadn't quite had the time to explain the ground rules to him.

There certainly hadn't been time during the night. She'd lost count of the times they'd made love. It was as if they'd stored up their hunger for each other for over a decade and it had suddenly broken free.

And this morning when she'd awakened, he'd been gone. There'd been a note on the pillow telling her that he'd had to get back for an eight o'clock class and reminding her that they were going to meet at one o'clock at the academy.

She felt a little pang that he'd left without awakening her. But she supposed that if you were an instructor at a military academy, one of the hard and fast rules was that you had to be on time for class.

She smiled. If he'd awakened her, she was pretty sure that he'd have been very late.

"Bianca?"

She turned to find Nicola giving her a quizzical look. "Sorry. Did you say something?"

"I just wanted to know what you thought of the church."

"And I was a million miles away." Marshalling her thoughts, Bianca glanced around the space.

"You're thinking about Nash," Nicola said. "Gabe told me that the two of you used to be an item."

"We're an item again." The words were out before she could stop them. But she didn't regret saying them.

"That's great. Gabe thinks the world of him. And so does my stepmother, Marcia. When I came back to Denver last fall, the first man she tried to set me up with was Nash."

Bianca's eyes widened. "Really?"

Nicola grinned at her. "Absolutely. He fits every one of Marcia's requirements. He comes from an established family. He even made the list of Denver's top ten most eligible bachelors."

"He did?"

"I kept a copy of the *Denver Post* article. I can show it to you. He looks great in a uniform."

It occurred to Bianca that aside from how great he looked in his uniform—not to mention out of it—she knew very little about the Nash Fortune of today. "Until

Maggie Fortune's party, I hadn't seen Nash for eleven years."

"It had been fifteen years when I met up with Gabe again. I fell for him even harder the second time around."

When Bianca said nothing, Nicola angled her head and studied her for a moment. "You're happy that the two of you are an item again, right?"

"Yes." That word was also out before she could prevent it. And it was true. She met Nicola's eyes. "Yes, I am."

"But it's scary. At least that's what I felt when Gabe and I reconnected."

"Scary as hell."

"I may have a solution for that. But first I have this problem—the one I dragged you all the way out here for."

As Nicola led the way into the church proper, Bianca turned her attention fully to her surroundings. The church of St. Francis was small and old-fashioned with a wide center aisle that drew the eye to the main altar. Behind it, a circular wall of stained-glass windows flooded the space with filtered sunlight.

"I can see why you wanted your wedding here," Bianca said. "The main altar is lovely."

"That's exactly what my stepmother says. She wants Gabe and me to be married right there in front of it."

Bianca turned to her. "And you don't."

"I want to make my vows to Gabe in front of the statue of St. Francis, and he's on the side altar. Let me show you." Nicola took Bianca's hand and drew her up the aisle and around the first row of pews.

Bianca saw the three tiers of candles first. Then she saw the statue of St. Francis under a glass dome.

She stopped short and felt her heart take a hard thump. "That's the same statue that used to stand in the prayer garden outside of the St. Francis Center for Boys."

"Yes." Nicola pulled her through the opening in the communion rail and up the steps to the altar. "It's always had this special power to answer prayers."

Bianca nodded. "I remember writing an article for the center's newsletter about that." She studied the marble statue—a slender man in a long brown robe with a gentle face and kind eyes. If she recalled what she'd written in the article, he was a saint who'd lived a quiet, prayerful life, who'd led by his example. And she'd have sworn she'd seen that same kindness in his eyes the night she'd tucked her "Dear John" letter to Nash beneath his feet.

"Well, the belief surrounding the statue's legendary power to answer prayers has grown since you left Denver. People come from all over on pilgrimages to this church just to say a prayer. There was an article in the *Denver Post* a while back that listed testimonials from politicians to newly engaged couples. They all claimed that saying a prayer to this statue changed their lives. It certainly changed Gabe's and mine."

Bianca turned to her then. "How did it do that?"

"It's a long story. We'll have to do a girls' night out sometime and I'll give you all the details. The short version is that I said a prayer to this statue when I was ten. I had a crush on Gabe, and I wanted to meet him again. Seven months ago we did meet again right in this very church." Nicola's cheeks flushed. "And I guess you could say we definitely reconnected."

Bianca took Nicola's hands and squeezed them. "Then, of course, you should be married on this altar. No brainer."

Nicola frowned. "Marcia is well-connected in Denver society. There will be hundreds of people invited. And the guests on the right side of the church won't have a good view of the side altar."

"Then don't let them sit there. Instead of separating the wedding attendees into bride's guests and groom's guests, just seat them all on one side. You can still walk up the main aisle and then cross over to this altar."

"You make it sound so simple," Nicola said. "Why didn't I think of that?"

"Because you're the bride. You have so many things to think about."

Nicola gave her a quick hug, then led the way down the altar steps. At the bottom, she paused and met Bianca's eyes. "Did you ever say a prayer to the statue when you were working at the St. Francis Center for Boys?"

Bianca nodded. "Once. It was just before my first newsletter came out. I was so worried."

"And it was great, wasn't it?"

"Yes." She smiled. "I still have a copy of it."

"Why don't you say another one today?"

Bianca glanced up at the statue. "I'm not sure what I want to pray for."

"Doesn't matter. Just say what's in your heart. He'll know what you mean."

Lifting her chin, she faced the statue. *Please let us find the right ground rules so that when we go our separate ways, we won't hurt each other again.*

Then she turned and walked with Nicola back down the center aisle.

11

THROUGH THE GLASS PANE in the classroom door, Bianca watched a young female cadet add something to a diagram that covered half the blackboard. Then her gaze was drawn to Nash, who sat on the side of his desk, his long legs crossed in front of him. Just the sight of that lean, rangy body had something deep within her taking a little leap.

Even in his present relaxed position, he emanated the strength and competence of a leader. There'd been some of that in the young man she'd known years ago. She supposed that it was an essential part of what had attracted her to him from the very beginning. But there was more now.

More of everything.

She let her gaze run over him again. From head to foot, he was an example of military neatness. His pants were creased, his shirt crisply ironed, every hair in place. She wanted badly to mess him up.

Down, girl.

For once she had to agree with that usually annoying voice. If she couldn't keep her mind off getting Nash out of that uniform, she was going to have the same problem establishing their ground rules as she'd had last night.

The cadet at the board turned to him, chalk still in hand. Though she couldn't hear through the closed door, whatever Nash said to her triggered a beaming smile, and the rest of the students in the class broke into applause.

As soon as the young woman returned to her seat, Nash said something and several hands shot up into the air. He pointed at another cadet, and the young man rose and walked to the board.

Nash didn't move. His position allowed him to easily switch his attention from the work at the board to the rest of the class and back again. He seemed very much at ease with his students and they with him.

That didn't surprise her. What did just a little bit was the sense she was getting that he was enjoying what he was doing. Did teaching hold the same attraction for him that flying always had? It was something she hadn't even thought to ask.

"Ms. Quinn."

Bianca recognized the voice even before she stepped back from the door and turned to face General Winslow. "General."

"I assume you're here to see Captain Fortune."

Heat rose to her cheeks. She felt as if she'd been caught with her hand in the cookie jar. "I have an appointment with him at one and I got here early. One of the cadets told me where I could find him."

"I was hoping to catch him after class." He glanced through the glass in the door. "Captain Fortune is well liked here at the academy. He's both an exceptional pilot and a talented teacher. He's an airman who is a credit to the Air Force."

"I'm sure he is."

"I was a classmate of his father's here at the academy so I've known him since he was a boy. Part of what makes him such a great fighter pilot is that he has good reflexes and good eyes. Those were what made him such an excellent quarterback for the Falcons. I watched him play several times."

"You were here when Nash played football?" His name hadn't appeared on the list that Jonah Stone had cross-referenced for them.

"Not at the academy. I have friends in the area. When I'm visiting Denver, I rarely miss a Falcons game. There were rumors that he could have turned pro, but I'm sure he never considered that. Being in the Air Force was always his dream. Did you know Nash has a medal of honor for saving the life of a fellow officer in Afghanistan?"

"No." There were lots of things she didn't know about Nash.

"Are you familiar with the term, wingman?"

She nodded.

"When one of the pilots Nash was flying with had to parachute out of his plane in enemy territory, Nash designed a strategy to fly in and rescue him. He got it approved, hand-picked the men he wanted to go in with him, and he pulled it off."

Pausing, General Winslow glanced through the glass into the classroom, then back at Bianca. "He has a tendency to think outside the box and take risks that more conservative officers would avoid. That can be an asset, but also a detriment to his career. I would hate to see anything or anyone interfere with the brilliant future he has ahead of him in the Air Force, especially when it means so much to him. His future is up to you."

He turned to her then and what she saw in his eyes had a sliver of fear working its way up her spine. "Nash is in need of a wingman now, and I think you know how you could fill that role."

Before Bianca could reply, the door of the classroom opened and students began to pour into the hallway.

General Winslow glanced at his watch. "Do me a favor. Let Nash know that I'll catch up with him later."

Bianca's stomach knotted as she watched the general walk away. He wouldn't have to catch up with Nash later. He'd made his threat very clear to her. If she had Nash's best interests at heart, she was supposed to back off on investigating Brian Silko's disappearance and make sure he did, too.

"You're early," Nash said. When she met his eyes, his narrowed. "And you're worried. What is it?"

"I just spoke with General Winslow. He said he'd catch up with you later."

"Really?" Nash cupped her elbow, drawing her back into his empty classroom and closing the door. "That's not all he said. Tell me everything."

When she'd finished, the smallest trace of a frown appeared on his forehead. "Interesting."

The knot in her stomach tightened. "Interesting? I didn't think when I asked you for help that it would put your career in jeopardy."

"It won't. It's an idle threat."

"No. There was something in his eyes. He's your superior officer. He has it in his power to affect your next promotion, your next assignment."

"He was also my father's roommate in college and his best friend. Plus, he's been a friend of my grandmother's for years. He just wants to scare you off. The question is why. He says that the initial investigations were thorough and there's nothing to find. If he's just worried about the reputation of the academy, why doesn't he just let you interview him and poke around to your heart's content? When you find there's nothing here, you'll just move on."

"Because there *is* something here." She felt that tingle deep inside that she'd felt from the moment she'd read that first anonymous note.

"I agree. I'm beginning to think the general has some idea of what it is. He wasn't teaching here at the time, but he was around."

"He just told me he has friends in the area. He caught some of your football games."

"I don't remember seeing him at all. But I'll check with my grandmother and see if he contacted her during that time. He'd think of her as a friend. Gabe is checking into the general's background. I'll ask Jonah to do a little digging also. If there's something there, one of them will find it."

She grabbed his hands. "In the meantime, we should probably be more discreet about meeting here at the academy."

"Not a chance. I'm your wingman now. And I have another idea about handling the general." He glanced at his watch. "I've arranged for us to meet Mac over at the airfield in ten minutes. C'mon."

Bianca had to lengthen her stride to keep up with him. "Nicola and I finished early, and I thought if I got here a little early, we could talk before we go to see Sergeant MacAuliffe. We didn't get a chance this morning."

When they stepped out of the building, a tour group blocked their way. Nash pulled her to a stop and turned to face her. "Before we have that talk, I need to do this."

He moved quickly then, pulling her into his arms and closing his mouth over hers.

I missed you. She wasn't sure if he'd muttered the words against her mouth or she'd just thought it. There was a part of her that wanted to push him away. To point out to him that they were standing in a public spot making a spectacle of themselves. But she did neither.

She was vaguely aware of the murmur of voices and muffled laughter, but she simply couldn't make herself care about that. It was only with Nash that she could be this way. He was the only one who could make her *feel* this way.

She placed her hands on his face to re-familiarize herself with the line of the bone, the strength of his jaw. As pleasure rippled through and needs began to throb, she inched up on her toes to get closer. Her heart began to pound so wildly, so loudly, she barely registered the applause.

It was Nash who pulled back and, keeping a firm arm around her shoulders, turned to the tour group they'd been entertaining and took a quick bow.

"I missed her," he said, grinning at them as he led her away.

They were nearly to her car before she said, "You enjoyed that, didn't you?"

"Immensely."

"I mean making a public spectacle of..."

"That, too."

She frowned. "It's going to get back to General Winslow that we... That you and I are..."

"An item?" They reached her car and he held out his hand for the key.

"Yes. I thought that we were going to be discreet."

"That was your idea." He opened the passenger door

and helped her inside. "While Gabe and Jonah are looking at his background, I'd like him to believe that our relationship is very personal and that we're constantly together because of that and not necessarily because I'm helping you dig up information on Brian Silko."

"Oh."

He grinned at her. "Pretty good plan, don't you think?"

By the time he'd climbed behind the wheel, she'd managed to gather her thoughts into a more coherent order. "One good plan deserves another, and I have one. It's about us."

"I have one, too. You first." He started the car and headed out of the parking lot.

She folded her hands in her lap and looked out the windshield. "I think that what happened between us last night was bound to happen. We're adults, we have a strong attraction to each other, and there's absolutely no reason not to enjoy the time we have to spend together."

Nash reached over and gave her clasped hands a quick squeeze. "I'm on the same page with you so far."

She looked at him then, studying that strong face that her hands had explored only minutes ago. "We just have to clarify the ground rules."

"Which are?" He took a right turn.

"What we have, what we share, can only be temporary."

Nash sounded the horn and waved as a young man passed them in a jeep. Bianca recognized the cadet who had met her at the gate on her previous visit.

"Temporary because?" he asked.

She drew in a deep breath and refocused her eyes through the windshield again. She could think more clearly when she wasn't looking at him. She'd gone over this part of her plan several times. First when she'd awakened and found that he'd gone without waking her, again in the shower, and a couple of more times during her drive to the academy.

"We're both here on a temporary basis—for work. When we finish our assignments, we'll leave. When that happens, I don't want to hurt you again. I don't want there to be any hard feelings."

Bianca paused, and when he said nothing to fill the silence, she said, "Do you agree?"

"It's a good plan."

Something tightened around her heart. The sensation was so sharp and so unexpected that she nearly pressed one of her hands against her chest. And that was ridiculous. His response was exactly what she wanted it to be. It *was* a good plan. A sensible one.

Nash turned onto a drive and pulled up to a gate. He showed his ID to the young airman on duty.

"Go right on in, Captain. Sergeant MacAuliffe is expecting you."

When he'd pulled into a parking space, she shifted in her seat. "So we're agreed?"

"You haven't heard my plan." Parking the car gave him time to push back the spurt of anger. They'd barely made a new start together and already she was planning an exit strategy. There was an irony in that because her strategy was one he'd used often with women before. Except for Bianca. And anger wasn't the way to solve this problem.

Turning, he fingered the loop of gold that dangled from her ear. "I know that you like to set goals. And as a pilot I can tell you that the goal is essential in any mission. But it has to be clearly defined. In our case, I don't see that it is."

She narrowed her gaze. "I think I explained it quite clearly."

"You explained two goals. Number one—we'll go our separate ways as soon as our assignments here come to an end. Number two—we don't hurt each other again, right?"

"Yes."

He stopped fiddling with the earring and moved his hand to the back of her neck. "There's a possibility that those goals might come into conflict. Plus, there's the added problem that sometimes while I'm in flight, I'll get new data that changes even a clearly defined goal. Then there's this."

Nash lowered his head as he pressed his hand more firmly against the back of hers. But he moved more slowly this time, giving her time to anticipate. Giving them both time. "I need to kiss you again."

It was nothing more than the truth. The taste he'd taken for the benefit of the tour group had only reminded him of how hard it had been to leave her room that morning. Even in his classroom, where he could usually lose himself in the lesson and in his student's discoveries, his mind had wandered to her more than once. No other woman had ever succeeded in distracting him that way.

No other woman had ever triggered this kind of hunger in him. "Just a taste. Something to tide us both over until we can be alone."

"We shouldn't. We need to make a rational decision about this."

"Shoulds and shouldn'ts didn't work for us before."

When she didn't move, didn't voice an objection, he

brushed his mouth over hers. Then, cupping the side of her face with his hand, he used his tongue to trace her lips before he slipped between them.

The instant her flavors began to pour into him, his intentions changed. New data totally blurred his goal. A sample was not going to be enough. How long had it been since he'd last tasted her? Minutes? An eternity? How had he managed to wait so long?

When she slipped her hand behind his head to draw him closer, he adjusted the angle of the kiss and took them both deeper. Ripe surrender was what he tasted now. Desire sharpened and needs built faster than anything he'd ever experienced even in flight. Only she could do this to him.

Only she.

Rationality evaporated and needs ruled. But as he tried to gather her closer, reality in the form of the gear shift console kicked in. They both were breathing hard when he managed to draw back.

For one instant the thought flashed brightly into his mind that he could easily shift both of them to the backseat.

"I want to touch you, Bianca. Really touch you."

"Not here." Her gaze shifted to the backseat. "We absolutely can't."

The fact that her mind was in tune with his gave him the strength to smile. "We could…. We have in the past."

"We were teenagers. It's broad daylight. Someone could come by."

"True." He deliberately shifted his gaze once more to the rear of the car and then back to her. "But why should teenagers have all the fun?"

"You're being ridiculous."

But her lips had twitched, and her voice was still breathless.

For a second, he said nothing, outrageously tempted. He'd parked at the back of the office building. They were fairly safe from prying eyes. Fairly. "I could convince you."

She lifted her chin and met his eyes. "How about this? I'll give you a rain check."

The offer was so unexpected, so delightful that Nash threw back his head and laughed. The Bianca he'd known eleven years ago would never have come up with that. He wouldn't have given her the opportunity. They'd have been in the backseat by now.

She smiled at him, and he realized it was the easiest, friendliest smile that she'd given him. "You've changed."

She narrowed her eyes. "I'm not so sure you have."

"Touché." He lifted her hand and pressed his lips against her knuckles. "I still have the car I drove the first time we made love."

Bianca stared at him. "You're not serious."

He crossed his heart with his finger and then raised his hand. "Swear. I store it in the garage at my grandmother's. We'll have to take a spin in it so I can collect my rain check."

Bianca didn't say a word as Nash got out of her car and circled around it to open her door. They'd made love in that car more than once. What could she say to a man who'd kept it all these years?

12

BIANCA WAS SURPRISED when instead of leading her into the building that sat adjacent to the airfield, Nash drew her toward a plane that sat on a nearby runway. "I thought we were here to see Sergeant MacAuliffe."

"He's over there climbing out of that plane."

Bianca spotted him the moment he started walking toward them. He was a tall man, thin as a gymnast with neatly cropped gray hair and sun glasses. Bianca guessed him to be in his mid-forties, and his face broke into a wide grin as soon as he saw Nash.

"Sergeant MacAuliffe, I'd like you to meet Bianca Quinn," Nash said.

"Call me Mac." He took off his sunglasses and shifted his gaze to Nash. "I haven't seen you in a few days and now I understand why. I brought your Cessna out just in case you want to take it up. Great day for it."

Nash smiled easily at him. "As tempting as the thought is, that's not why we're here. Bianca writes true crime stories and she's researching the disappearance of Cadet Brian Silko. I recalled you were here working at the airfield when it happened."

Mac's expression immediately sobered as he looked at

Bianca. "I was here. I'm not sure I can tell you anything I didn't tell the police, but we can go into my office."

He continued to talk to Bianca as they walked. "I was assigned to aircraft maintenance at the time. I worked on the plane that Cadet Silko stole. It was a honey."

He led the way into the building Nash had parked behind. His office was small but pristine in its neatness except for a tall pile of folders on his desk. More surprising was the aquarium teeming with tropical fish that filled one corner of the room.

Mac gestured them to a small conference table. "Would you like coffee? I can guarantee it's strong and hot."

"No thanks," Bianca said.

As soon as Nash refused the offer, Mac joined them at the table and addressed Bianca. "What do you want to know about Cadet Silko's disappearance?"

Bianca took a small notebook out of her bag. "How well did you know him?"

"I knew him almost as well as I knew Nash here. There are always new cadets at the academy who like to hang around the airfield every chance they get. The planes are what attracted them to this branch of the service. For Nash it was the flying. Brian liked the maintenance side as well as the flying. A couple of times when he was hanging around, I let him watch when I was working on a plane."

Bianca jotted down a few notes, then asked, "What was he like?"

"Nice kid. But very quiet. Any conversations we had focused mostly on what I was doing to a plane and why."

Bianca met Mac's eyes. "Do you have any idea why he stole the plane?"

Mac leaned back in his chair. "My gut reaction when I first heard about it was that he simply hadn't done it."

"Your second reaction?" Nash asked.

"He might have done it for a girl." He raised a hand. "I don't have any proof of that. But when I got to thinking about it, I recalled an odd conversation we'd had. He told me a story about a close friend of his who'd fallen hard for a young woman. Her family was against it, so they had to sneak around to be together. Then his friend found out that the girl was going to have to go away with her family. He'd never see her again. Unless he ran away with her."

Bianca's hand tightened on her pen. "You think he was talking about himself."

"I didn't at the time. The officials here at the academy and the police conducted separate investigations. I didn't even mention it the first few times I was questioned. It was only when the policeman, a Detective Loomis, I believe, specifically asked me if there might be a girlfriend involved that I remembered the conversation."

Mac smiled. "Loomis was one of those policemen like you see on TV sometimes—the kind who kept coming back and picking at things, the way you might pick at a bothersome scab. I finally told him about it."

Bianca glanced at Nash. "Odd. There was no mention of a girlfriend in the report Loomis wrote up." She turned back to Mac. "Can you remember how many times Detective Loomis came back?"

Mac considered. "Four, maybe five times. I'm surprised he didn't make mention of it in his report. He impressed me as being thorough."

"Do you think Brian crashed the plane?" Nash asked.

"Loomis asked the same question. I'm not sure we'll ever know. But I don't think so. The wreckage was never found. But even with the kind of resources they had available to them, neither the Air Force nor the police ever discovered where that plane might have refueled."

"Right," Nash said thoughtfully. "There are lots of places to land a plane, but it's more difficult to get fuel without a record being kept."

"Unless he had a friend somewhere. I mentioned that to Loomis last time he talked with me. Brian knew his way around planes. He had to have come by that knowledge some place."

Bianca studied him. "Do you think he's still alive?"

"I hoped at the time that it was a possibility." He shrugged. "But it's been over ten years."

There was a knock at the door and a young woman poked her head in. "Your appointment is here."

Bianca tucked her notebook into her purse as she and Nash rose. "Thank you so much."

"You're going to look for him, aren't you?" Mac asked.

"Yes."

"Let me know what you find."

"You'll be the first to know. I'll also see you get a signed copy of Bianca's book," Nash said. "And I'm going to take my plane up after all."

"Enjoy," Mac called after them as they left.

"WE ARE NOT GOING for a plane ride," Bianca said as soon as they were out on the sidewalk.

"We need to think. At least, I do, and I do some of my best thinking in the cockpit."

"We need to track down Detective Loomis and find out why he didn't put the possibility of a girlfriend in his report. Plus I'd like to know his theory about Brian Silko's disappearance."

"I thought you said he was retired. Do you even know where he lives now?"

"No, they weren't very helpful at the station, but—"

"I'll give Gabe a call. His firm is good at tracking people down." He punched numbers into his cell phone. "While he's doing that you can plan the questions you're going to ask Loomis."

He was right, she decided as she listened to him give Gabe the name and what they wanted. He glanced at her. "Gabe wants us to join Nicola and him and Jonah at Jonah's new club around 8:00. He thinks he can have the information you want by then."

To her surprise, he handed the phone to her. "Nicola wants to talk to you."

She took the cell. "Hi, Nicola."

"Hi, Bianca. I'm calling about that pendant you were wearing last night. Remember I said I thought I'd seen some jewelry that was similar? I described it to my stepmother and she remembered exactly where we'd seen some pieces with that cob-webby design. It was in a boutique jewelry shop called Caprice—it's downtown near the Museum of Art. I can text you the address if you'd like."

Bianca fingered the pendant. Maybe it was bringing her good luck. "Thanks, Nicola. I'd definitely like the address of that shop. I'll check it out."

"What will you check out?" Nash asked as he cupped her elbow and led her through the gate.

Bianca dug in her heels. "Nicola told me where I might find out something further about the pendant I found in your grandmother's attic. The one I'm wearing."

He turned to study it. "You think it has some connection to Jeremiah?"

"I do. It was with that photo. The styling is very

distinct, and Nicola remembers seeing similar pieces there. If we can't visit Detective Loomis this afternoon, I could at least go there. She says it's right near the Denver Museum of Art."

"Then we'll go. Later this afternoon," Nash insisted as he urged her toward the small plane sitting on the runway. "You know what they say about all work and no play. When was the last time you did something just for the fun of it?"

She opened her mouth and shut it as the memory came flooding back. Those were the exact words he'd said to her the first time he'd invited her to take a ride with him in his car—a flashy little convertible, the one he'd held on to all these years. She could see in his eyes that he'd used the words deliberately so that she would remember. "Nash, it's not the same. We can't go back. We're both different now."

"I agree. Aren't you curious about how different we've become? When we find out, maybe we can go forward."

Fear warred with hope inside of her.

Smiling, he held out a hand. "All I'm inviting you to do is take a break, have some fun. Come fly with me?"

Her heart took a little tumble as she put her hand in his and let him guide her up the steps and into the plane.

"YOU'VE DONE IT AGAIN," Bianca said as the small Cessna climbed into a bright summer sky.

"Takeoff's the easiest part." Perfectly at home behind the controls, Nash spared her a glance and noted that she was gripping the edge of her seat.

"I'm not talking about the takeoff. I'm talking about how I let you talk me into doing things that I really shouldn't be doing."

Nash grinned. "It's my pleasure. But this is new. I've never talked you into going up in a plane with me before."

As the land tilted away beneath them, a tricky patch of crosscurrents set the plane rocking. Bianca caught her breath and tightened her grip on the seat.

"Everything's fine," Nash said. "As soon as we get up high enough, we'll have a smooth ride."

She said nothing as he banked to the right and continued to climb, but Nash noted that she'd squeezed her eyes shut.

"You don't like planes," he said. "I never knew that before."

"I like planes just fine. I'm just used to big ones where I can't see all the controls and there isn't all this noise. I always choose an aisle seat and work."

Nash shook his head. He had to show her how much fun it was to fly.

But first he had to distract her. "Once Gabe tracks him down, what will you ask Detective Loomis?"

"I want to know why he kept coming back to question Mac. There has to be something that bothered him. And I want to know why he suddenly dropped it and why there was no mention of a possible girlfriend in his report. Suddenly dropping the case doesn't fit with the kind of cop Mac described."

"I agree." Though she hadn't opened her eyes, her hands weren't gripping the seat quite so tightly.

A few moments later, he leveled the plane off. Below, everything was green—peaks to the north and wide flat valleys between. They were flying low enough to see cars along the highways and little clusters of houses. "Take a peek. You'll never get this kind of view from a passenger jet."

Drawing in a deep breath, Bianca opened her eyes and glanced out the window. For the next few minutes, silence stretched between them. Then she said, "How often do you come up here?"

"As often as I can. Sometimes I take a few of my cadets up with me, but mostly I come up here alone."

She shifted her gaze to him. "Do you miss it? Flying combat missions, I mean?"

"I do. But I wanted a change. This is how I get my fix."

Nash could still feel the tension radiating off of her. To distract her, he said, "If you look out to your right, you'll see the church of St. Francis."

"Yes, I see it. Nicola and I visited there this morning. She wanted my advice on something about the wedding." As the small church passed out of her sightline, she turned back to Nash. "Did you ever say a prayer to the statue when you were a boy?"

"Sure. Father Mike made Gabe, Jonah and me all say one soon after we all started going there."

"What did you pray for?"

"At that time my sole goal in life was to follow in my father's footsteps—graduate from the Air Force Academy, become a fighter pilot." He shot her a grin. "I think I might have even tagged on a prayer that I would become a hero."

"He answered all your prayers."

"You could say that." He glanced at her. "How about you? Did you ever pray to the statue?"

"Once. I prayed my first newsletter would be a success." She smiled. "I forgot to add on that I wanted to become a published writer and a heroine."

Nash laughed. "Father Mike always said that St. Francis would hear what was in our hearts."

"That's exactly what Nicola said to me this morning."

"She ought to know. St. Francis, both the statue and the saint, played a huge role in bringing her and Gabe together. I'm thinking that must have been in both of their hearts. They're perfect for each other." He gestured to the window on her side. "Look over there. You can just see the same river we saw when we had that impromptu picnic."

For the first time, Bianca realized that she'd stopped gripping the edge of her seat and that she was beginning to relax. "How long do you usually spend when you come up here?"

"It varies. There are so many times when I've taken a plane up with a specific mission that I like to make up my mind as I go."

She looked at him then. "Is this the kind of plane that Brian Silko stole?"

"The one he took was bigger—one of those executive-style ones that you see in the movies. Why?"

"It occurred to me that if a girl played a role in his disappearance, she might have been with him. Ever since Mac told us his theory, I keep thinking if he's right, she had the courage to do what I didn't."

Nash reached out and took her hand. "I've been thinking the same thing about Brian."

"But you're not the one who lacked the courage. I'm the one who left the note and ran away."

"I'm the one who didn't come after you." He banked the plane to the left and headed east. "So the way I see it, when it comes courage or the lack of it, we're even." As the wings leveled out, he spared her a glance. "If you could, would you go back and change things?"

"I don't think so. That's why I'm worried about us now. That's why we should lay out some kind of ground rules. You're military. Surely you can see the advantage of having a strategy."

"Definitely."

The plane hit a little bump and Bianca glanced out the window. Her stomach took a dip when she saw the ground was closer. "What's happening?"

"We just hit some cross currents. There may be a few more before we land."

"Land?"

She scanned the ground beneath her, but all she saw was peaks and narrow valleys. "I don't see an airport."

"There isn't one. Keep an eye out. See that peak up ahead."

"Yes." She saw it all right. They were heading straight for it. Her stomach plummeted.

"Once we get past it, keep a look out for a flat space."

Bianca held her breath as he nosed the plane up and over the peak. Then she scanned the ground. It was getting close enough that she could make out individual tree tops.

"There it is. Can you see it over there?"

She could barely make it out—a narrow ribbon of land cutting through the trees.

"Hang on."

She already was. Nash banked the plane and took it lower. Hills shot up on either side of them now and the land rushed toward them. He maneuvered the plane with the same precision as if he were threading a needle.

"Now."

She sucked in a breath as the wheels thudded hard, then expelled it when they bounced, teetered and finally rolled to a stop.

13

SHE TURNED TO HIM. "You're crazy."

He grinned at her. "My grandmother would agree with you."

"And I must be crazy to have ever agreed to get in this plane with you. We were supposed to just fly around."

"We did fly around."

"You wanted to think."

"I still do."

How could she want to shake him and laugh at the same time? *Sensible,* she reminded herself. One of them should at least try. "We have leads we could be following."

"That's the problem. You're going to want to visit that shop near the museum today. Then when Gabe tracks down Detective Loomis, we'll have to visit him. I have classes to prep, and any spare time you have you'll tuck yourself away in my grandmother's attic to see if you can find any more clues to Jeremiah's story." He lifted her hand and pressed his lips to her fingers. "I'm calling a time-out."

"For what?" But she saw the answer in his eyes before he even spoke. Her eyes narrowed. "You dragged me all the way out here and landed on a microscopic sliver of dirt so that you can collect on a rain check?"

His brows rose. "You were the one who gave it to me. And we'll get to that. But my primary purpose in bringing you here is that I want to spend some time with you. Away from the stories you're tracking down."

"Tracking down stories is my job. It's who I am." But her argument sounded weak, even to her own ears. He'd always been able to surprise her, and that had always delighted her.

"Everyone needs to take a break. And I want to show you something." He held out a hand.

Her hand was already reaching toward his, but as their fingers touched, she tried for some damage control. "I'll go with you, but we have to settle our ground rules before we leave here today."

"Deal."

Bianca followed him out of the plane. Once she got her feet on solid ground, she discovered that the view was magnificent. The narrow stretch of flat land was cupped perfectly between two mountains that rose steeply into high peaks. Directly in front of them the land curved and a narrow canyon forked to their right.

"It's not far," Nash promised as he led her into the canyon. They walked in silence, their fingers linked. As the strip of sky narrowed overhead, Bianca heard the water, a gentle murmur at first, but it grew steadily louder until the canyon took a sharp turn to the left, and there it was. From high up on the canyon wall, water gushed and tumbled over and around the rocks until it splashed gently into a wide pool. It stretched about fifty feet in front of them before narrowing into a stream that disappeared around the next curve.

"It's lovely. How did you ever discover it?"

"This is another one of those spots my father brought me to before he left for the Gulf War. It's my favorite. He told me he used to bring my mother here, and he wanted me to know about it."

She turned to study his profile as he watched the sunlight glisten off the pool. "You still miss him."

"Yeah." He turned to her then. "I was furious when he didn't come back. I gave my grandmother a hell of a time. 'Acting out' is what the school psychologists called it. She called it taking after the black sheep side of the family."

"Your great-great-great-uncle Jeremiah."

"Yeah." He glanced around before he returned his gaze to hers. "I haven't been back here since I came to teach at the academy. And I've never brought anyone else here. Not even Jonah and Gabe."

Something tightened around her heart, and his hand gripped hers as if he sensed the urge she had to step back. "My ground rules are simple, Bianca. I want to spend time with you. I want to get to know the woman you've become."

"You're going to find I'm still different. We're both still different."

"So? Opposites attract."

She jerked on her hand, but found it held fast. "Our past history shows it's not that simple. And we have the same problem we had when we were teenagers. Our careers are essential to us. I go where the story takes me. You go where the Air Force sends you. We're going to eventually go our separate ways just as we did before."

"You could be right, but you're not considering a very important thing."

"What?"

"I teach my students that ground rules are essential in any team effort and especially on a mission. Everyone has to know them and agree to them. But they're a starting point. They may have to be modified as the mission goes forward."

She narrowed her eyes. "You've not going to agree to my rules, are you."

"I absolutely am—as long as you know that sometimes the ground rules have to be modified or renegotiated. And sometimes new ones have to be added."

She studied him for a minute. "Only if we both agree."

"Absolutely. Now I want to propose my first addition to the ground rules. In addition to enjoying each other, I want to explore what we have together and see where it leads. How does that sound?"

Wonderful. Scary.

"I don't think either of us should harbor unreasonable expectations."

The recklessness flashed into his eyes for only a second, but she couldn't prevent the thrill that moved through her. She expected him to end the discussion by kissing her. There was a part of her that wanted him to. Desperately.

"The only problem I can see is that we might have different ideas about just what an unreasonable expectation is. I don't want to shut down any options. And I think you still do. So why don't we settle it this way?"

Once again, she expected him to pull her into his arms and end their discussion the same way he'd ended it before their meeting with Mac. Instead, he released her hands and she had to stifle a surge of disappointment when he stooped over to select a stone from the ground.

With a flick of his wrist, he sent it skipping over the surface of the pond.

"Are you any good at skipping stones?" he asked.

She leaned over, selected her own and then sent it sailing toward the water. It hit the surface three times before it sank.

Nash grinned. "Don't tell me your aunt Molly taught you to do that as well as play poker."

"She did. When we first moved to the Boston area, we used to take long walks along the Charles River."

"I'll give credit to my grandmother's tutoring for this one." Nash's next shot also hit three times. "What's your personal record?"

"Let me show you." This time she spent more time in her selection. When she found what she was looking for, she straightened and sent it off. It skipped six times before sinking. "Not my best. One time I made eight."

His next stone skipped six times. "I'd say we're evenly matched, wouldn't you?"

"I suppose."

"So here's the deal. We'll each take one shot. If you win, we go with your plan—no unreasonable expectations. If I win, then we simply have more options."

If she refused, they were at a stand still. It was the most she was going to get from him, and she was pretty sure she could win.

"What do you say?" Nash asked.

"You're on." She stooped over and ran her hand over the tumble of rocks and dirt that bordered the pool. Finally she picked up the flat stone, flicked her wrist a few times. And then sent it flying. It skipped along the surface of the pool seven times before it sank. "Your turn."

For a moment, Nash hesitated. She was grinning at

him, totally delighted at what she'd just done. Her eyes were sparkling, and he wondered if she'd ever looked more beautiful. And if he kissed her now, he could make her forget what they'd talked about. More than that, he could demonstrate just how unreasonable his expectations were. But he didn't teach a class in strategic planning for nothing. And if he didn't throw his stone, she could claim victory by default.

Leaning down, he poked around in the scattered stones just as she had. The one he selected was roughly triangular in shape, flat but thicker in the middle so that the edges narrowed like the wings of a fighter plane. When he rose, he didn't look at Bianca. Instead, he focused on the pool and pictured just what he wanted the stone to do.

Then he sent his missile sailing. In the seconds that it took to hit the water for the first time, he found himself saying a prayer to St. Francis. Something he'd hadn't done in years. Then he held his breath and counted the skips. Two—three—four—five—six—seven. For an instant, he thought that would be it, but the stone took to the air for one last maneuver before it hit two more times.

The look Bianca gave him was a mix of amusement and admiration. "I think I was just conned."

He shrugged. "I do have more training in aeronautics than you do." Plus he'd said that prayer. He took both of her hands and met her eyes. "One thing I can promise you. I'm going to make us both winners. And if we do go our separate ways, we'll do it better this time."

"I guess I can live with that." Then she looped her arms around his neck. "There's just one other thing."

"What?"

"I think you should collect on that rain check now."

It was both surprise and desire that she saw in his eyes, and it was the former that gave her the biggest thrill.

"It would be my pleasure," he said.

Their lips were still an inch apart as they lowered to their knees. Neither of them closed the distance as they began to undress each other. She struggled with buttons while he dealt expertly with straps and zippers. Her sundress was pooled around her knees by the time she'd tugged his shirt free of his slacks.

His fingers were at the clasp of her bra when she leaned away. "You're faster at this than I am. Let me catch up."

"Gladly."

She slipped her hands beneath the opening of his shirt and shoved the material away, drawing it down his arms until it reached his wrists. When he made a move to free himself, she said, "Wait. I just want to look at you."

He eased back on his heels, and she ran her gaze over the hard planes and angles of his body from shoulder to waist. "I feel as if I've just unwrapped a present."

Then she ran her gaze over him again, taking in the sinewy muscles at his shoulders, the smooth skin stretched taut over his chest and abs, the narrow waist. When her gaze lingered there, she saw the movement of his muscles, heard the quick catch of his breath. Power moved through her.

Raising her eyes to meet his, she ran her finger along his waist just where she'd been looking and experienced a fresh thrill when he shuddered.

Inches still separated their lips, but when he moved forward, she avoided the contact. If he kissed her now, she'd be lost.

"Not yet." Meeting his eyes, she said, "When I get

involved in a research project, I like to linger with the evidence, examine it very carefully. Right now I want to confirm that you feel as good as you look."

"Go ahead." His voice was rough and the feeling of power built.

With her eyes still on his, she raised her hands to his shoulders, then, spreading her palms flat, she ran them slowly down his chest, this time absorbing the bristly silk of his hair, the hard pebbles of his nipples, and the hard ridges of his abs.

She liked the contrasts in textures, even the way her skin looked pale compared to his. But it was his reactions—the hard thud of his heart against her palm, the ragged sound of his breath, that had heat building to the flashpoint inside of her.

"Bianca, I want you."

It would be so easy to just close the distance between them, to cover his mouth with hers and surrender. But that was the pattern she'd always followed. So instead, she looped her arms around his neck and smiled. "I know you want me. I can see it in your eyes. They're dark, almost as dark as the sky just before night falls. But they get even darker when you're inside me."

His breath caught then and in one swift movement he rid himself of his shirt and settled his hands at her waist. "Why don't you unwrap the rest of the present?"

"You said you wanted time with me to explore. I want the same with you." She ran a finger over his lips, testing their firmness.

What he wanted was to have her. Now. But even as the urgency of his desire grew, he didn't move. She'd never teased him this way before, and he was mesmerized. The realization that she could enchant him left him burning and weak. And wanting. "Let me taste you."

"Not yet. Research is a slow process."

His fingers tightened their grip on her waist. "Taste me then."

Keeping her hands firm on his shoulders, she leaned close enough to trace the path her fingers had taken with her tongue. Greed rose swiftly, painfully, and the temptation to shove her to the ground and take her spiked until he wasn't sure how much longer he could control it. But warring with it was an equally strong desire to see just what she would do next.

As if she read his mind, she took one of his hands from her waist and pressed her lips to his palm. "I like your hands. I love the way they feel on my skin."

"Say the word."

"Soon." Leaning in, she nipped his bottom lip. "I like your mouth even more. Whenever you kiss me, I can't think of anything but having you inside of me."

It was the second time she'd mentioned having him inside of her and he knew what it would feel like. He could already feel her tight hot core taking him in, enclosing him and pulling him deeper and deeper.

"I want to kiss you so much. Eve must have felt just this way in the Garden of Eden. No wonder she tossed paradise away."

"Bianca, you're running out of time."

"Really?"

Nash wondered for an instant who made the move. In that first meeting of lips, he couldn't have said who was the aggressor. Then his mind emptied and filled only with her and the need to make her his. He lifted her so that she was straddling his thighs. With his mouth still fused to hers, he made quick work of the barriers that still separated them.

He wanted, no, he needed to touch her everywhere.

But there wasn't time. There wasn't even time for finesse while her mouth was on his, seeking, finding, exploiting. Together they tore at his belt and the clasp of his slacks until they freed him. And all the while, her taste flooded him, her hands tormented him to go faster.

Time ran out as he lifted her hips and then his own to plunge into her. And she was right with him, driving him as furiously as he drove her until he knew nothing else. Only her. Until the world shattered around him.

WHEN HE FINALLY SURFACED, Nash found himself lying on the ground with Bianca pressed closely against him. Each time he drew in a breath, it burned his lungs. And he was sure he could hear the pounding of his heart above the noise the water fall was making.

What had she done to him? He'd never taken any woman with less control. He didn't even have any clear idea of how they'd ended up on the ground. Had he hurt her?

Dazed, he levered himself up enough to meet her eyes. They were half-open and fixed on his. Incredibly, he felt a fresh stab of desire. He should move away before he took her again like a mad man.

"Are you all right?" she asked.

"I think so. You?"

Her lips curved. "I'm not sure I can move my toes yet."

Her smile triggered a warmth deep inside of him. "I'm not sure I can move my own." He hadn't tried to move them. Truth told, he didn't want to move at all. Propping his head on his hand, he studied her, and it occurred to him that he would have been happy to stay right where he was on the hard ground—as long as she was there, too.

"This isn't exactly what I had planned."

"I think it's exactly what you had planned, Captain. Mission accomplished."

The dryness of her tone surprised a laugh out of him. "Touché." But his expression sobered almost immediately. "I have a condom in my pocket that I didn't use."

"No problem. I'm on the pill."

Then as more of his brain cells began to click back on, he studied her more thoughtfully. "You wanted to drive me crazy, didn't you?"

"I did drive you crazy."

The mix of satisfaction and triumph he saw in her eyes had him smiling. He wanted badly to drive her crazy right back. For hours. At nineteen, that's exactly what he would have done.

But now he wanted more. For both of them. He took a strand of her hair and wound it around his finger. "Come home with me tonight."

"What?"

"I know that you have a perfectly good hotel room, and as fond as I am of it, I'd like you to spend the night at my place."

"Why?"

He leaned down and brushed a kiss on her lips. She had a knack for asking the tough question. The truth was he wanted her there. In his home. But he wasn't sure she was ready to hear that yet. "It's closer to the academy, and it will give us more time. Plus, we can make popcorn, watch old movies, neck on the sofa, all those things we didn't do last time around."

He could see the capitulation in her eyes, but it was followed by pain.

"Ouch."

He got to her knees and drew her up so that he could look at her shoulder. While they'd been making love, the pendant had slipped to the back of her neck. "No blood." He studied it as he shifted it around. "You're right about the distinctive styling. It's very unique. Maybe you're right and it will lead us to more information about Jeremiah Fortune."

"I know it will. I have a feeling. I felt it from the minute I found this pendant in that box in the attic. I just have to find out what the story is. That's why we have to get back to Denver and get to that shop before it closes."

"I don't suppose I could talk you into skipping more stones."

She met his eyes. "I know just what you want to talk me into. But you'll just have to take another rain check."

Nash rose to his feet, pulled her into his arms and spun her around in a circle.

Bianca's head was still spinning when he set her on her feet. "You're a surprising woman, Bianca Quinn. I'm beginning to like you very much."

Then he surprised her by picking up her sundress and tossing it to her. "Last one dressed has to make the popcorn tonight."

14

"HURRY," BIANCA SAID as they left Nash's car in a parking lot across from the museum. The bright yellow awning sporting the name Caprice had caught her eye immediately when they'd driven past it.

"We have nearly half an hour before the shops close," Nash pointed out.

Before they'd left the little canyon, Nash had suggested that they rinse off in the pool. It had been a good idea, but the process had delayed them enough that they'd hit traffic when they'd neared Denver.

She stopped the instant they reached the window. The minimalist but tasteful display might have caught her eye even if she hadn't been specifically coming here. A framed water color hung over a table set with hand blown glass and colorful pottery. A beautifully woven throw covered a chair, but it was the carved chest of drawers that had her stepping so close that she nearly pressed her nose against the glass.

On it sat an overflowing jewelry box. But none of the pieces were what she was looking for.

"Over here," Nash said, pointing to a second window. There on a glass topped table were a necklace and set of earrings. She'd decided against wearing the pendant, but she took it out of her purse to compare. Both pieces on display were silver and the lacy pattern of the design was reminiscent of the pendant. "It's not exact, but it's no wonder Nicola made the connection. Let's go in. Surely, they can tell us how to get in touch with the designer."

The moment that Bianca stepped into the shop, she stopped short. She felt Nash tense at her side, but she couldn't take her eyes off the young girl standing behind the counter. Her first thought was that she had to be mistaken. Her eyes were still adjusting from the bright sunlight out on the street.

But the long dark hair and the slender build were so similar. When the young girl glanced up at her, she saw the same surprise that she was sure was on her own face.

"Bianca Quinn. You're really here." She hurried around the counter. "Does that mean... Tell me it means that you've decided to look into my brother's disappearance?"

"Your brother?" Nash asked.

"Brian Silko. He's my older brother. Oh, I'm sorry. I'm just so excited that you're here." She held out her hand. "I'm Marianne Silko."

"Marianne," Bianca said as she shook the girl's hand.

"You *are* here to investigate my brother's disappearance, right?"

"I am looking into Brian's disappearance. Captain Fortune is helping me."

"Captain Nash Fortune?"

"Yes," Nash said.

"My mom took me to the football games that Brian played in so I saw you a few times. Brian said that you were one of the best quarterbacks the Falcons had had in years."

Bianca turned to Nash. "I believe Marianne is the young woman who left me an anonymous note at my book signing in Chicago. You also mailed my editor and me the notes, right?"

"Yes."

The bell over the shop jingled and two women walked in. Marianne beamed a smile at them. "Welcome to Caprice. I'll be right with you."

Turning back to Bianca, she spoke in a low tone. "I can close the shop in fifteen minutes. Can you wait? There's a nice café across the street."

"We'll meet you there," Bianca said.

On their way out, Nash nudged her over to a display case. Inside, a pendant on a fine silver chain lay on a swirl of velvet. The one she'd found in the attic was much older, the silver duller. She took it from her purse and placed it on the counter. The one in the case lacked the turquoise stones of the older one, but there was no mistaking that the intricate design of the scrollwork was similar.

Nash tapped a finger on the top of the case, and Bianca shifted her gaze to the folded card in front of the piece. It contained a picture and the name of the designer. Marianne Silko.

THE SMALL CAFÉ ACROSS from Caprice was noisy and crowded. Customers who'd dropped in for a drink after work mingled with the early-dinner crowd. Ten minutes after he and Bianca had snagged a table by the window, Marianne joined them. Since then, Nash had decided that he was in the presence of a top notch interviewer. It wasn't that Marianne wasn't willing to share information. She was. It was keeping her on track that was the problem. And Bianca had managed to do that in the same quiet and focused way she played poker.

Between the time they'd given the waitress their order and the drinks had arrived, Bianca had managed to finesse an amazing amount of background information out of the young woman. He remembered Nicola's remark at his grandmother's birthday party about wanting to hire Bianca for the FBI, and he thought Gabe's fiancée might be on to something.

Marianne's mother had died in the spring after a long illness, but there'd been enough money from the sale of their home to bankroll Marianne's college expenses. She'd just finished her freshman year at the University of Colorado, and her career goal was to become a jewelry designer, something that she'd been pursuing since her grandmother first taught her how to work with silver. As a result of winning a statewide competition in high school, her jewelry was already being carried in a few high-end boutiques like Caprice.

Her summer job at the small shop was a paid internship, and in return for working extra hours, the owner allowed her to use the equipment in the back of the store to work on her own designs.

Nash sipped his coffee. The two women were a study in contrasts. Marianne was outgoing and she exuded energy. She perched on the edge of her chair and used her hands when she talked.

Bianca had energy, a lot of it, but she kept it more carefully controlled and focused. She seldom made gestures when she talked. The only thing she was using her hands for was to record a few notes.

She'd been taking notes the first time he'd seen her through the window of the St. Francis Center. He'd been drawn to her even then in a way that he'd never experienced before. When she'd looked up and met his eyes, well, that had been it for him. He hadn't realized it at the time, not even when she'd run away. But he knew it this time around. She was still the one for him.

He wanted to tell her. He wanted to shout it. But he'd have to wait. He'd promised her time.

As Marianne swallowed the last of her soft drink, Nash signaled the waitress for another round. Bianca set down her pen, took out the pendant and placed it in the center of the table.

"Before I ask you any specific questions about your brother, I'd like you to look at this. The reason that Captain Fortune and I came to your shop today was to find out information about it. A friend of mine said the pendant reminded her of some pieces she saw at Caprice. I believe she must have been talking about your designs."

Marianne examined the old pendant carefully. "Whoever designed this was a skilled craftsman." She ran her finger along the weblike design that joined the turquoise stones. "It's so delicate. My grandmother instructed me in this technique, but I'm still working at mastering it."

"Did your mother design jewelry also?" Bianca asked.

Marianne smiled. "No. She was a nurse. She always said that she never inherited the design gene. My grandmother left me a collection of pieces that had been passed down to her. I use them sometimes to inspire my designs. I'd like to compare this pendant to some of those pieces. I'll bring them with me to the store tomorrow."

"I'll stop by and we can look at them together."

Bianca tucked the pendant back into her purse. "Now I have another question for you. Why all the secrecy? Why did you send me anonymous notes?"

"I saw one of your interviews on television. The interviewer asked you if you had a new project in the works. You said that you had been bombarded with suggestions—over twenty emails a day—and that you hadn't yet had the time to sort through them all. In another interview you mentioned that you had started digging into the story for *Cover Up* when you received an anonymous tip."

Bianca's eyes widened. "I do remember saying those things."

"I thought that sending you the notes might get your attention and intrigue you."

Bianca smiled slowly at the girl. "Well, it certainly did. You got my editor's attention, too. But why me?"

"My mother read your book when it first came out. She remembered that you'd gone to junior high school with Brian and you'd written a profile on him for the school newspaper. When she was finished with *Cover Up,* I also read it. It was incredible. You found out things that no one else had. The police had closed the case. You opened it up again, and you discovered the truth." She leaned forward. "That's how I know that you're the person who can find my brother."

"You believe he's alive," Bianca said. "Or did you say that in your third note just to further intrigue me?"

"I *know* he's alive. And I have proof." She reached into her purse and pulled out a brown envelope. "After my mother died, I had to clean out the house. I found these in a shoebox at the back of her closet. Now I carry them with me all the time to keep Brian close."

Marianne placed a stack of photos on the table.

"There are ten of them, one for each Christmas since my brother disappeared."

Bianca picked up the stack of photos and passed them to Nash after she'd studied each one. He examined the first one carefully. There was a couple smiling at the camera. They stood on a beach. Behind them some rocks jutted out into the water. It could be an ocean or a large lake. The Merry Christmas message was printed in the green border below the picture. He examined the next two, then met Bianca's eyes. "It's Brian, all right." He glanced at Marianne. "Do you know who the woman is?"

"No."

"The year he disappeared—did he have a girlfriend?" Nash asked.

Marianne bit her lip. "I've thought about that. I was eight when he disappeared. But I remember the police asked my mother and me that question. She told them that she suspected he had found someone because he wasn't coming home to Phoenix as often. But she didn't have proof and she couldn't give them a name."

Nash glanced back down again at the second picture. The girl had curly brown hair, and wore it longer than in the first one. She was shorter than Brian and slim. Pretty rather than beautiful. In the third photo, there was a baby. They held the infant between them as they once more smiled into the camera. In the sixth photo that Bianca passed him, there was a second child, and the first one, clearly a boy, came up to Brian's waist. In the ninth one there was a new baby in a frilly pink dress. When he'd looked at the last one, Nash met Marianne's eyes. The ten Christmas photos told a story of a family that was growing, seemingly thriving. And they looked to be very happy. "Brian is not only alive, but it looks as though you have a nephew and two nieces. Your mother never told you about any of this?"

She shook her head, and for the first time he saw a trace of tears in her eyes. She had her hands clasped tightly in front of her. "Never. And those pictures are all I have. I searched through everything. There's nothing else."

"You have no idea how your mother got hold of these pictures? No envelopes?" Bianca asked.

"Nothing. Just the photos. All these years, Brian's been alive and I didn't know. I took the pictures to the police station in Colorado Springs shortly after I found them, and I talked to a detective. He said that there wasn't enough here to reopen the case. He explained that I couldn't even prove that these are of Brian. But they are."

"I agree," Nash said.

Marianne looked from Bianca to Nash and back to Bianca again. "Will you please help me?"

Bianca reached for her hand and linked her fingers with the young girl's. "Yes. We will."

"Do you think you can find out why my mother kept this secret all these years?"

"We're going to try," Bianca said.

To Nash's way of thinking, Marianne had just given voice to the million dollar question.

IT WAS A LITTLE AFTER EIGHT when they reached Jonah's new club, Passions. From the glimpse she got of the main dining room, Bianca thought it was well-named. The ceiling was studded with starlike lights and black pedestal tables surrounded a two tiered dance floor. But it was the bar that drew her attention as Nash threaded them through the crowd waiting for tables.

A long slab of gleaming black granite formed a huge horseshoe in the center of a long room. It offered chrome seating for what looked like a regiment of guests, and nearly every chair was filled. Black leather booths hugged the walls and mirrored panels reflected light and images of a crowd that looked to be a mix of both suited-up business people and tourists. The flat-screen TVs hanging at intervals from the ceilings were muted and the recorded music was low enough to encourage conversations as people sipped their drinks and nibbled at food.

"This place has both comfort and style," Bianca said.

"Jonah's good at providing both," Nash said. "I think I see our table."

Bianca spotted Nicola waving at them from a booth at the far end of the bar.

Gabe rose and pulled up extra chairs to make room for them.

"Jonah, this is spectacular," Bianca said as she slid into a seat next to him.

"You should see the two clubs he already has in San Francisco. And now he has a business partner in Rome." Nicola offered a tray of appetizers. "Jonah wants us to sample these. Try the shrimp first. They're the newest addition to the menu. The restaurant here has already received a rave review in the *Denver Post*."

Bianca selected one without any more urging.

"You've got yourself another gold mine here," Nash said.

Jonah grinned at him as he passed him a beer. "That's the idea."

"I ordered white wine for you," Nicola said as she pushed it toward Bianca.

Once the tray of food had made its way around the table, Gabe said, "Since I called this meeting, why don't I go first? Not that I have much to report. "General Winslow has no family living in the Denver area. He had an older brother John who lived in Atlanta with a wife and two kids, a daughter seventeen and a son thirteen, but they disappeared from the area twelve years ago. I haven't been able to locate them. But they're not around here in Denver. I've tracked down retired Detective Loomis of the Colorado Springs police who handled the first investigation into Brian Silko's disappearance. I tried tracing him through his license plate, but when he sold his house two years ago, he never bothered to update his address. The young man I put on it visited the Colorado Springs police department."

"None of them could tell me where Loomis lived," Bianca said. "Or they wouldn't tell me. My feeling was that they didn't want him bothered."

"My man used the story that he needed to contact Loomis because he'd come into some money. It's an old ploy, but in this case effective. An older sergeant remembered that Detective Loomis owned a cabin near Boulder. We found him through registered deeds."

Gabe glanced from Nash to Bianca. "I had my man go up and scout the place out. Loomis is there, but I told my man not to make contact. I thought you might want to visit him yourself."

"Thanks," Nash said. "We'll drive out there first thing in the morning. We have even more interesting news." He turned to Bianca. "You tell it."

"We found out that Brian Silko is definitely alive." She pulled out the Christmas card pictures, laid them face up in the center of the table. Then she brought them up to date on how they'd accidentally run into Brian's sister, Marianne, and what they'd discovered or tried to deduce so far.

For a moment after she'd finished, none of them said a word. Nicola was picking up each photo and examining it carefully, then passing them on to Gabe and finally Jonah.

"It's the woman we're interested in," Bianca said. "Both Sergeant MacAuliffe and Marianne's mother had hunches that Brian was seeing someone. But it was a secret. He never brought the girl home."

"A secret romance and a sudden disappearance. You think they may have eloped together like Romeo and Juliet?" Nicola asked.

There was a moment of silence at the table. Bianca stole a glance at Nash and saw Jonah and Gabe exchanging looks with him also. "It's one explanation," she said.

"There are easier ways to run off together than stealing a plane," Jonah pointed out. "And from the field at the Air Force Academy. It triggered a lot of press coverage." He turned to Nash and said, "How did you and Bianca plan to elope?"

Nash met Bianca's eyes. "Car. We were going to drive to Vegas."

"Really? How romantic," Nicola said.

Nash kept his gaze steady on Bianca. "But we intended to come back. We weren't going to disappear for the rest of our lives."

"Only one of you *did* disappear and that was before the elopement." Jonah picked up a shrimp, but looked Bianca directly in the eye. "What's the plan this time?"

Bianca met his eyes squarely. "We're working on it."

"Good." Jonah popped the shrimp into his mouth.

Nicola covered Bianca's hand with hers. "Don't you pay any mind to Jonah. He was just as obnoxious to me when I started seeing Gabe. He looks like this tough guy, but he has this inner mother hen thing going."

"Jonah does have a point about the plane," Nash said. "By stealing it, Brian created a big story. The press was focused on it for weeks. And because no one found any bodies or any record of it landing anywhere to refuel, everyone believed it crashed and his body was never recovered."

Bianca met his eyes. "So what *weren't* the press and the police focused on?"

"Exactly," Nash said. "What else was going on?"

"If Mrs. Silko's and Mac's hunches are right, there's a girl who disappeared also," Bianca pointed out. "Someone must have reported her missing."

"I'll put some of my people on that." Gabe pulled out his cell. "If someone else disappeared in the area, there should be a record in the newspapers or in police reports."

Nash leaned back in his chair while Gabe spoke into his cell. "There's another thing about the plane."

"What?" Bianca asked.

"Brian loved them. He joined the Air Force to fly. If he had to give that up…" Nash paused for a moment. "If I'd had to give up being in the Air Force, I'd never have been able to give up flying. That could be another reason why he took the plane."

He leaned forward and turned one of the latest photos around to study it. "He had to give up his mother and sister. And a future in the Air Force. But he looks happy. I'm betting he didn't give up everything about his old life. He's still flying."

Bianca leaned back in the booth. "He literally gave

up one family for another one." She turned to face Nash. "If I'd run away with you, we wouldn't have had to make that choice. We planned to come back to Denver and make a home here. Aunt Molly and your grandmother wouldn't have been happy."

"But they would have taken us back, helped us out," Nash said.

"Maybe that wasn't a possibility for Brian. We don't know anything about the girl's family," Bianca said. "Maybe there would be no forgiveness there. Maybe they had no choice but to cut themselves off completely."

"So sad," Nicola murmured. "But love is a powerful motivator."

"You're biased," Jonah pointed out. "The other powerful ones are greed and survival. I'm betting there's more than love going on here."

Nash studied Bianca as his friends batted around theories of why a young couple might have had to make such a difficult and drastic decision. He found himself enjoying the way the lights played on her features. It occurred to him that he could have been happy to look at her just this way for a long time. Without getting restless. Or bored.

Why hadn't be been as certain of that at nineteen? If he had, he would have gone after her. He glanced down at the photos. Brian had been certain. And he thought of the photo that Bianca had found tucked in the pages of the old journal. If Jeremiah had chosen that woman over his brother, he must have been certain, too.

When he glanced up, he saw that Bianca was studying the same photo. When she met his eyes, he saw both understanding and sadness in hers.

Progress, he thought. And it wasn't just on the case that they were making it. She was wondering, too, what they'd missed. But what they had to focus on was what they could have now. And he wasn't going to able to wait much longer to tell her that. To convince her of that.

"So what do you think, Nash?" Jonah asked.

Taking a moment to gather his thoughts, Nash glanced down at the photos again. "I think there's a love story at the heart of it, but there's more."

"There has to be more to have caused General Winslow's veiled threats," Bianca said.

"Threats?" Jonah asked. "What kind of threats?"

"He's hinted that if I don't stop poking into this story that Nash's career may hit a few stumbling blocks." Bianca turned to Nash. "After we talk to Detective Loomis, I think we ought to have a chat with General Winslow and ask him why he wants me to back off."

"In the meantime, why don't I help Gabe track down General Winslow's older brother—the one who disappeared so suddenly from Atlanta?" Jonah offered. "That may give you some leverage when you talk with the general." He glanced over at Gabe. "I'll bet I get the information before you do."

Laughing, Gabe raised both hands palms out. "Do I look like someone who would take a sucker bet?"

"On that note, I'm taking my fiancé to the dance floor." Nicola winked at Bianca. "I highly recommend it."

Jonah rose. "I'm going to circulate among my guests. And I'll let you know as soon as I find something."

Bianca gathered up the photos and placed them carefully in her purse.

Nash captured her chin in his fingers and tipped her face up so that he could see her eyes. "Why do you think Brian stole that plane?"

"I don't have a coherent theory yet. But I agree with

you. There's something more than a love story going on. Otherwise why all the secrecy?" She glanced down at the photos. "Why have they had to remain hidden all these years?"

"What if the secret has to remain buried? What if you can't write it?"

"I'm not prepared to consider that yet. First I need to find the whole story, and I'm more convinced than ever, that there's a hell of a one here. It looks like Brian and the girl both gave up a lot to build the life they have together." She met his eyes. "But if I can't tell their story, I'll just have to be satisfied with writing Jeremiah Fortune's story."

He moved slowly, leaning in so that she could avoid him if she wanted. When she didn't turn her head away, a knot of tension he wasn't even aware of eased inside of him.

They kept their eyes open as their mouths met and separated, then met again to cling. There was a sweetness here that was new, a flavor that he didn't ever recall sampling before. A warmth, sweet and slow-moving as honey, seeped through him until it permeated everything he was.

And when she framed his face with her hands, and softened against him, yielded completely, he knew that he couldn't, he wouldn't let her go.

Not this time.

Not ever.

When he finally drew back, her eyes were half-closed, but still on his. "Let's go," she said.

"Don't you want to try out the dance floor?"

"I believe that earlier you invited me back to your place."

Nash felt his heart take a long fall. He captured her

hand in his and drew her out of the booth. "We're on our way."

"There's just one place I want to stop first."

15

"YOU'VE INFECTED ME," Bianca said as she turned on the ignition. "I'm now just as crazy as you are."

"I couldn't be happier." Nash fastened his seat belt as she drove the small sports car out of his grandmother's garage.

He'd been surprised when she'd asked him to drive to the Fortune Mansion. But utter astonishment was the phrase for what he'd felt when she'd revealed that they were stopping there only to switch his car for the Porsche. And she wanted to drive.

So at ten at night, she was behind the wheel of the sporty little convertible that he'd driven when they were first dating eleven years ago. And she was making quick work of the curving drive that led away from his grandmother's house.

"You're stealing my moves," he said. "I'm the one who should have thought of switching cars."

She shot him a look. "Who says you always have to be the one to make the moves?"

He grinned at her, delighted. "Who indeed?"

"Someone's watching us from the house. They'll probably call the police."

He craned his neck and saw that the light was on in his grandmother's room on the second floor, and he saw two silhouettes in the window. "Relax. Grady recognized the code I punched into the gate." He decided against telling her that his grandmother was also watching their escape, probably with a great deal of satisfaction.

When they reached the front gate, Nash keyed it in again and the gate swung open. But it wasn't until she'd negotiated two stop signs and hit the gas pedal to shoot the car through a yellow light that he leaned back in his seat. "You've had some practice using five gears."

She smiled at him before she downshifted and shot the car up a ramp. "I've had some practice driving a Porsche. I put a down payment on one with the first royalty check from my book."

He stared at her. "You bought a Porsche."

"I loved yours, and I always envied the ease with which you drove it. So when I had enough money, I couldn't resist."

"You're a surprising woman, Bianca. Are you going to tell me where we're headed?"

"Your place. Eventually."

"Let me know when you need directions." He leaned forward and punched a button. Paul McCartney and John Lennon's voices surrounded them, singing, "I saw her standing there."

He heard her quick intake of breath, and as they drove beneath a streetlight, he had the satisfaction of seeing that her knuckles had whitened on the steering wheel.

"You kept the tape," she murmured. It was the first present he'd ever given her—an album of the Beatles' greatest hits. They'd played it constantly whenever they'd stolen enough time to be together.

"You're a surprising man, Nash Fortune."

They drove in silence for a bit. For the time being, it was enough to just fly through the night with the wind blowing at them and the music swirling around them. The memories were there, but Nash didn't want to indulge in them. What he wanted was to capture the present. He was so engrossed in just watching her drive and living in the moment he didn't register where she'd been headed until she pulled onto a narrow road that led upward into the hills.

"This isn't the way to my place," he commented as she turned down the narrow dirt driveway. The no trespassing sign was still nailed to a tree.

"You said that the land was yours."

It was. He'd inherited it when his grandfather had died. But he hadn't been back here in eleven years.

When she pulled the car into the clearing and stopped, neither of them spoke for a minute. Then he said, "Why did you bring me here?"

She turned to face him. "Because I want to make love to you here where we first made love."

"Why?"

"I asked myself that three times on the way up here. And three times I told myself that I could simply stay on the highway to Colorado Springs. But I couldn't keep my hands from making the turns."

He lifted her hands from the wheel and pressed first one and then the other to his lips. "I guess I owe them."

She lifted her chin and met his eyes. "And I owe both of us a better reason than that one. Those pictures. When we were looking at them with Marianne, what I saw was proof that the feeling I had about this story was right. But when I was looking at them in Jonah's club, what I saw was the ten years of happiness that Brian and his lover have shared. The most recent picture with the three kids—they look even happier than they did in the first. I couldn't help but think of what we might have walked away from."

"I thought of the same things," Nash admitted. "But we wouldn't be the same people we are today."

"No. And I'm not saying I have regrets. It's just…I don't know what tomorrow will bring. But looking at those pictures makes me want to savor what we can have right now in the moment."

Nash felt his heart take another long tumble.

"Can we just do that?" she asked. "Can we just think about this moment and not worry about the future?"

"We can." He climbed out of the car and circled it to help her out. Then pulling a lever, he opened the trunk. "I still have the blanket."

She smiled at him. "I was banking on it."

Hands joined, they walked to the far edge of the clearing. Beyond it, the land tumbled away. Nash spread the blanket on the ground. Their eyes were locked as they worked on their clothes. Once again, he worked faster, but eventually they both stood naked in the starlight.

She took his hands and raised first one and then the other to her lips. "Make love with me?" she asked, repeating the exact words he'd said to her on that long ago night.

"Yes."

Enjoying the way his eyes darkened, she drew him down with her, shifting at the last moment so that she lay along the top of him. "Do you remember how you kissed me that night?"

"I remember."

"So softly. Like this." She brushed her mouth against the tip of his nose, his cheeks, and finally his lips. "You were so gentle, so tender. You told me how much you liked my taste."

She nipped at his bottom lip. "I like yours, too."

When he reached for her, she linked her fingers with his. "I was nervous, but you soothed all the nerves away with pleasure. You made me float." She continued to taste him, sliding down his body to nibble at his throat. Pleased when he didn't resist, she continued to tease them both, building desire slowly just as he'd done for her.

His skin was cooler along his shoulders, warmer on his chest. She liked the sensation of his heart pounding against her lips and the way his stomach trembled when she ran her tongue along the taut, smooth skin at his waist. His scent, his flavors, poured into her. They were becoming familiar again, a part of her.

She felt the fire begin to build inside of her, but it was smoldering rather than blazing.

Weakness. Nash felt it burn through his system, melting everything in its path. She was enchanting him. He didn't try to fight it.

Her lips were so soft as they returned to sample his again. Her fingers grazed his skin leaving a path of fire and ice in their wake. Stars glittered overhead, and the music from the car radio thrummed in his blood.

Everywhere she touched, he trembled, yielded. She could take whatever she wanted. But she gave as much as she took. There seemed to be no end to her generosity.

Finally, he found the strength to raise his hands to frame her face. Then he just looked and looked and looked. Slowly, almost painfully, she lowered her head until their lips met again, then parted, and met to cling.

"Now."

He wasn't sure who said the word or if it was only a wish. But he glided his hands down to her hips, lifted her and then slid into her.

She rose and their fingers linked again as their bodies fused more fully together.

Time spun out, and when they finally moved it was in unison, slowly, until greed finally took over and swept them away.

THE NEXT MORNING, they set off early to find Detective Loomis.

"The cabin should be right ahead." Nerves danced in Bianca's stomach as Nash eased the Porsche around yet another bend.

Nothing but trees and yet another curve faced them. The road, if it could have been called that, had turned to gravel about a mile back. Gabe's man had said Detective Loomis's cabin was isolated, but they hadn't passed another house in the past fifteen minutes of driving.

Nash shot a look at her. "You're nervous. Do you want me to question him?"

"No. It's just that so much depends on his answers." She hadn't let herself think of the interview during the night. She hadn't let herself think of anything during the night except Nash.

"Just handle it the way you usually handle an interview. Your strategy works."

She glanced at him. "I'm not sure I have one. It's the one part of my life where I sort of have to feel my way."

"While you were drinking your coffee, I saw the list of questions you jotted down in your notebook." He down shifted as the next sharp curve approached.

"But I have to be ready to change them based on what he says. An interview is always tricky that way."

"That's exactly what I was trying to explain to you about flying a mission. You have to react and adjust based on new data."

"I suppose."

He shot her a grin. "I'm beginning to think we're a lot more alike than we're different."

The problem was she was beginning to think so, too. And perhaps that was the reason for the nerves that had been dancing in her system ever since she'd left the shower that morning. In spite of all of her efforts there was a part of history that *was* repeating itself. The more time she spent with Nash, the more she wanted to be with him all the time.

And that wasn't going to be possible.

"Here it is." Nash slowed the car and pulled it to the edge of a clearing. The cabin was a small A-frame tucked into the rocky hillside. As she climbed out of the car, Bianca took in more details. The cabin boasted a porch and a wide picture window that looked out over rolling green hills and darker valleys.

On the grass in front, a tall man turned away from an easel, and the dog at his side, a huge spotted creature, lumbered to his feet and loped toward them barking.

"Barney, stay!"

The rich baritone voice stilled the dog at once—except for the tail which continued to wag.

The man set a brush and palette down on a small table before striding toward them. As he did, Nash squeezed her hand and spoke in a low tone. "Remember, I'm your wingman. Just let me know if you want me to play good cop to your bad cop."

She barely suppressed a laugh. "You do remember

that this is an ex-cop we're dealing with. I think he'd recognize the ploy."

"Just trying to help."

Retired Detective Ted Loomis was tall and thin with a shock of gray hair. He looked more like an amateur artist than a cop. He appeared amiable enough, but his eyes were shrewd, and Bianca doubted that he missed a thing.

"You don't look as if you've come to sell me anything," he said as he halted a few feet away.

"We haven't," Bianca said.

"Don't tell me I've really inherited a substantial sum from a relative I'm sure I don't have."

"No...oh!" Bianca raised a hand to her forehead. "A man who works for Gabe Wilder used that story at the Colorado Springs Police Department to track you down."

"And the sergeant who talked to him called me to let me know right after he let it slip that I owned a cabin in the Boulder area." He glanced at Nash, then back to Bianca. "Gabe Wilder of G.W. Securities? Do the two of you work for him?"

"No. This is Captain Nash Fortune and I'm Bianca Quinn. We want to ask you some questions about your investigation into Cadet Brian Silko's disappearance."

Loomis's eyes narrowed on her. "You're the writer. And you were at the Colorado Springs Police Department a few days ago reading the files on that case. My friend mentioned you when he called about my sudden inheritance. Everything I know is in my report."

Bianca met his eyes. They gave nothing away. Beside her, Nash said nothing.

"If there's nothing else," Loomis said, "I'd like to get back to my painting."

If she was going to get anything out of Loomis, she was going to have to give him what she knew. "I don't think you did put everything in your report. Captain Fortune and I have spoken with Sergeant MacAuliffe. I also have information from Brian's sister, Marianne. I've seen proof that Brian Silko is alive. I think you know or suspect that he is, too."

Loomis's eyes narrowed. "What kind of proof?"

"Photos of Brian and his family. Ten years' worth. I think he's still with the young woman you suspected stole that plane with him. I intend to find him. I need to know if you think there's a good enough reason why I shouldn't."

There was a moment when Nash thought he might continue to stonewall them. Then Loomis smiled slowly. "Why don't I make us some coffee. I'll want to see those pictures if you have them, and then I'll tell you what I know."

Fifteen minutes later, they were gathered around a table in front of the picture window sipping coffee. Bianca had given as precise a report as he'd ever heard on what they knew so far from Marianne. She'd left out any speculation they had about General Winslow, but she'd shared everything else.

Loomis had to have been as impressed as he was with her report because he said, "I'll tell you what I know, which isn't all that much. Once I talked with MacAuliffe, I had a hunch that some girl had played a key role in Silko's disappearance. I even discovered her name—Paula Harwood. She was eighteen and attending a high school in Denver along with a brother who was four years her junior. But by the time I tracked her address down, there was no trace of her, the brother or the parents. Neighbors said they'd been gone about a week."

"About the same amount of time that Cadet Silko had been missing," Nash said.

"Exactly. The same day I discovered the family had disappeared, I was paid a visit by US Marshals. They don't tell you very much, but they badly wanted me to back off. What they were willing to share was that Paula's family had been relocated in Denver through the witness protection program, and they'd had to be suddenly relocated again. I was told that if I continued to try and find out where Paula Harwood was, I could endanger all of their lives."

Bianca's mind began to race. When she met Nash's eyes, she knew his mind had taken the same leap that hers had. One year earlier, General Winslow's brother's family had disappeared from Atlanta. Could they have been relocated to Denver? She turned to Loomis. "So Brian and this Paula are in witness protection with the rest of the Harwoods?"

"No," Loomis said. "That's the interesting thing. From what I could read between the lines, Paula was supposed to disappear with her family, but at the last minute she decided to run off with Brian. She was that determined to be with him. In the words of the marshal I talked to, it would be better for everyone if any and all interested parties believed that Paula was with her family. They didn't want either Silko or Paula found."

"So you backed off," Nash said.

Loomis shrugged. "Without the girl, I didn't have any other leads to follow. The plane Silko stole was insured. The Air Force wanted the media attention to die down. And I guess I figured the kids and that family needed a break." He shifted his gaze to Nash and then back to Bianca. "Are you going to try to find Brian and Paula?"

"I don't know," Bianca said. "While I've been looking into Brian's disappearance, this is the second family I've come across that's vanished without a trace—husband and wife with two teenaged kids. The first family disappeared from Atlanta a dozen years ago."

"And a year later the Harwoods disappeared from Denver," Loomis mused. "Could be a coincidence, but you think there's a connection?"

Bianca glanced at Nash. "If the Harwoods were relocated from Atlanta to Denver and then something here triggered another relocation…"

"It could be the same family," Nash finished. "Paula Harwood could be the same girl who disappeared from Atlanta a year earlier."

"I have to check it out," Bianca said.

With a smile, Loomis nodded at her. "I'd do the same in your shoes. Good luck."

As she picked up the photos, he said, "Do me a favor. If you can, let me know how it all turns out."

"We'll do that," Nash promised.

NASH'S CELL PHONE RANG as they pulled into a parking lot near the art museum. He and Bianca had been on their cell phones ever since they'd left Loomis's cabin. He'd filled Gabe in on the possibility that the young woman Brian had run off with could be General Winslow's niece, and Bianca had told Nicola everything they'd learned. She was going to ask her father, who headed up the Denver FBI office, to see what he could find out. If anyone could get more information on the Harwood and Winslow families, FBI agent Nick Guthrie could.

His cell continued to ring insistently as he stopped the car. After checking the caller ID, he said, "Grams, you're home."

"You know very well I'm home. You spotted me in the window last night before I had a chance to duck out of sight. And you're in trouble."

He flicked Bianca a glance. "On the bright side, I'm not bored anymore."

He thought he heard a stifled snort of laughter on the other end of the phone. "I've just talked to General Winslow, and he didn't sound happy. He'd like to speak with both you and Bianca. I told him I was meeting with Bianca this afternoon and that I'd arrange for you to be present. He'll be here at 2:00 p.m."

"We'll see you then."

After pocketing the phone, he climbed out of the car and joined her as she started across the parking lot. "General Winslow is meeting us at my grandmother's at 2:00."

"That will save us the trouble of tracking him down. How much damage can he do to your career?"

Nash shrugged. "We may change his mind if we tell him what we discovered. We have a name now. And if the Harwood family turns out to be the Winslow family that disappeared from Atlanta—if Paula Harwood is his niece and we show him those pictures…"

"He could still very well tell you that your temporary teaching assignment at the academy has been terminated."

He stopped at the edge of the street and turned her toward him. "We don't know what will happen. There's no way to predict it. We don't have all the data yet." Then he leaned down and brushed his mouth over hers.

It was just the briefest of contacts, but Bianca couldn't

stop her arms from winding around him. Nor could she stop herself from leaning in and taking more. Sunshine poured down on them, people streamed by on the sidewalk, but for the moment she let herself do what she'd been wanting to do ever since she'd left him in the shower that morning. She just held on to him as if she never wanted to let him go.

A few hand claps from a passer by had her gathering herself and drawing back.

"Bianca?"

She saw the question in his eyes, and she knew it was the same question that had her nerves dancing again. But she didn't know the answer. "We have to see Marianne."

They started down the street toward Caprice. "The problem is, Detective Loomis has me thinking along the same lines as General Winslow. Loomis is a good cop. And he had a good chance of finding Brian. But he walked away. And I don't know what to tell Marianne about her brother."

Nash linked his fingers with hers. "You don't have to tell her anything at this point. You're doing the best you can on this. Gabe is checking into the Winslow family that disappeared from Atlanta. Nicola's father has been in the FBI for a long time and he has connections. Plus, he has the names Winslow and Harwood to work with. There's a good chance that he'll be able to fill in some of the blanks for us. In the meantime, the reason you're seeing Marianne this morning is because of that piece of jewelry."

"Right. I'd nearly forgotten." She stopped and turned to give him a quick hug. "Thanks. And that's why I'm meeting with your grandmother today—to give her a report on how I'm doing so far on the Jeremiah story."

Nash couldn't have named the flood of emotions she'd triggered in him with that one sweet gesture. But it took him two beats to catch up with her as she strode with new purpose toward the shop.

Marianne was ringing up a customer, but she gave them a wave the instant they entered the store. They barely had time to walk over to the counter before the customer was on her way and Marianne joined them.

"This is some of the jewelry that my grandmother passed on to me when she died." Marianne retrieved a box from under the counter and opened it. "Some of them are pieces she was given by her aunt and her grandmother."

There were a dozen or more pieces of silver jewelry in the box, and as Marianne laid them out on the counter, Bianca's eye kept returning to one particular necklace. The silver hammered links were the size of nickels and hanging from them was a trio of stones framed in the same lattice like design of the pendant. It was older than the others, and tarnish had darkened some of the more intricately chiseled silver.

Reaching into her bag, she pulled out the pendant she'd found in the attic. The design wasn't exact. But it was close. And the turquoise stones set in the center of the discs had the same sky-blue clarity that the ones in the pendant had.

Marianne tapped her finger next to the necklace that had first caught Bianca's eye. "I knew that you'd be interested in this one."

"I am. It's older than the others, isn't it?" Bianca asked.

"Yes. And it has stones similar to your pendant. My grandmother always said that it was her inspiration piece,"

Marianne explained. "This one's mine. My grandmother made it for my mother, and she left it to me."

Bianca glanced at the piece that Marianne held up. She could see the influence of the young woman's inspiration piece in the collection of jewelry in the display case. She studied the necklace. "I can also see the influence of this older necklace in your work."

"Jewelry making has a long history in my family. The tribe has always believed that certain techniques, like the method of twisting the fine wires of silver into webs of lace, have to be passed on to the next generation. And the techniques developed in the new generation also have to be handed down."

"You said your tribe," Bianca said.

"Yes, my great-grandfather's father was part Navajo. He was raised on a reservation and his daughter, my grandmother, learned some of the techniques before they moved away. At least that's the story my grandmother told me. And in addition to the pieces of jewelry she'd been given, she also had this journal."

Marianne reached into the box and brought out what looked to be a handmade book. The cover and binding were made of leather, and the uneven pages were yellow with age.

Bianca linked her fingers with Nash's and held on hard, but even when she felt him glance at her, she kept her eyes on the journal. It was nearly an exact match to the one she'd found the pendant and the photo in.

"My grandmother told me the story of Falling Star when I was very young," Marianne said. "She fell in love with a white man and when they married, she ran away from the tribe. Later, when her husband died, she returned to her people with the child she was carrying.

Falling Star designed my grandmother's inspiration piece. And I think she also designed your pendant."

Marianna opened the book carefully to one of the first pages. "Look."

Bianca's heart took a leap when she glanced down at the page. They were filled with sketches of jewelry designs—some rough, others more finished. But her eyes stopped on one and her heart leaped again. She laid the pendant next to the sketch. A perfect match.

Nash's fingers tightened on hers as she met Marianne's eyes again. "You said that Falling Star left her tribe to marry a white man. Do you know what his name was?"

Marianne's brow furrowed. Then she carefully opened the book to a later page and began to run her finger down the lines of script. Turning the page carefully, she scanned it. "I'll find it."

Bianca glanced at Nash while they waited. But she had the same feeling that she'd had when she'd first opened that old box in the attic. And she knew what his name would be.

"From what I remember of the story my grandmother told me, they were very much in love, but their story didn't end happily. He was a prospector and he'd found a rich vein of gold. On the day he went into town to get supplies and register the claim, he was arrested for stealing a horse and he was hung, his claim stolen. My grandmother said that a good friend of his brought Falling Star back to her tribe. Ah, here it is," Marianne said triumphantly. "She called him Jeremiah."

For a moment, Bianca said nothing. She couldn't take her eyes off the journal and the pendant.

It was Nash who spoke. "Marianne, would you trust

us to take the journal with us? I can guarantee that we'll take good care of it, and you'll get it back."

"That's fine. It's such a coincidence that you have that pendant. It looks as if it might have been made by Falling Star."

"Yes," Bianca said as she tucked the pendant back into her purse. Then she carefully closed the journal and picked it up.

The bell jangled over the door and three young women came into the shop. "I'll be with you in a sec," Marianne called out to them, and she carefully restored the pieces in her grandmother's box.

As she settled the last one in, Bianca took her hand. "We're working on finding your brother. I don't know if we will."

Marianne met her eyes. "I know you'll do your best. I knew that when I sent you those notes."

Bianca waited until they were out on the street before she said, "If Falling Star was pregnant with Jeremiah's child when she returned to the reservation and Marianne and Brian are her descendents, then…" Stopping, she glanced down at the journal in her hands. "The records have to be checked, of course, but you know what this means. You could be related to Brian and Marianne Silko."

"Yes." Nash raised her free hand to his lips. "You know what else it means?"

She met his eyes. "What?"

"Jeremiah's and Brian's stories are linked in more ways than one. Not only are they related, but they both had the courage to follow their hearts and risk everything to be with the woman they loved."

16

AN HOUR LATER, they sat in Maggie Fortune's office at Fortune Mansion. Bianca knew the room well. She'd signed that old agreement here. But it wasn't a contract that lay on the gleaming mahogany conference table this time. It was ten Christmas pictures that were spread face up across the surface. Above them was the blank journal and the newspapers Bianca had retrieved from the attic. Below the pictures of Brian and his family was the journal Marianne had given them.

She'd shown Maggie the pendant she'd found in the attic and laid it next to the sketch in the journal.

Bianca'd had time to skim through the pages on the drive over and she'd read aloud the pertinent parts to Nash. Marianne had hit most of the highlights. But in the earlier entries, Falling Star had written about her guilt and sadness over the fact that she had been the cause of Jeremiah's estrangement from his brother, Thaddeus. Since their wedding, Jeremiah had been schooling her in English, and she'd used the journal to record the events of their lives together. The pages were filled with joy and hope for the future. She was designing jewelry, Jeremiah had discovered gold, and they would be bringing a new life into the world come spring.

There was no mention of Jeremiah's death, no mention of Falling Star's return to her tribe. Those parts of the story must have been passed along to her descendents through word of mouth.

Maggie Fortune stood with her hands flat on the table, skimming through the pages in the journal. When she finished, she picked up the pendant again. "Well, I think there's ample evidence that the Jeremiah referred to in this journal is our Jeremiah. There can't be two of them who fought with a Thaddeus over a woman. Plus, there's the journal from the attic which exactly matches the one that Marianne gave you and the pendant. Now we know that Jeremiah wasn't really a horse thief. I'm betting the men who hung him trumped up the charge to steal the map to the new vein of gold he'd discovered."

"That's not a bad theory," Nash said.

"I've been wondering how a blank journal and the pendant as well as the newspaper articles ended up in the attic with Thaddeus's things," Bianca said.

"Good question," Maggie said.

"Perhaps Falling Star contacted Thaddeus after Jeremiah's death," Bianca said. "She felt guilty about splitting them up. She might have wanted Jeremiah's family to know what had happened to him."

Maggie met her eyes. "That's not a bad theory, either." Then she set the pendant down and fisted her hands on her hips. "One thing I know for certain—I've opened up a regular Pandora's box, haven't I?"

Bianca blinked. It was not the reaction she'd expected. She glanced at Nash and saw that he was grinning.

"Serves you right, Grams."

Maggie pointed a finger at him. "Don't you dare say 'I told you so.'"

Nash pantomimed locking his lips and throwing the key away.

Baffled, Bianca looked from one to the other of them. "Why is this discovery about Jeremiah a Pandora's box? I know there is still a lot to discover. But we can start in Indian Springs. There'll have to be a death certificate."

Maggie waved a hand. "It's a Pandora's box because it means Falling Star's descendants are part of the Fortune family. Jeremiah may have had a falling-out with Thaddeus and run off to prospect on his own, but the fact remains that he owned half of the gold mine that created the Fortune family's wealth. All these years, we've been operating under the false assumption that he hadn't had any offspring. Now we learn that his wife was pregnant when she returned to her tribe, and Marianne Silko and the missing Brian may be descendants of her child. Of course, I'll have to have my lawyers check it all out. But the evidence here—" she paused to wave at the book "—is substantial, and they deserve their share of the profits from that original mine. At the very least."

"Look at the bright side, Grams," Nash said. "Your lawyers will get some hefty bonuses working overtime, and there may be someone in the mix—" he pointed to the pictures "—who can one day take over the company so that you can finally retire."

"First we have to find Brian," Maggie said.

"That's where it gets sticky." He recounted what they learned about Brian Silko's disappearance so far.

She narrowed her eyes. "Witness protection. I'll give Nick Guthrie a call."

"Nicola has already asked him to see what he can

find out. But if Detective Loomis is right and Brian and Paula ran away so that she wouldn't have to disappear with her family, then they're not in the Witness Protection Program. They're on their own."

Maggie frowned down at the photos. "Brian probably inherited that 'running away and starting over' gene directly from Jeremiah."

Nash narrowed his eyes on her.

"What?" she asked.

"I've got a theory this time." He pointed a finger at her. "You set this all up, didn't you? Only you got more than you bargained for."

Eyes wide, Maggie pressed a hand to her chest. "I don't know what you're trying to imply."

Nash began to tick things off on his fingers. "One, you decide that Jeremiah's story has to be told. Two, you decide that Bianca is the perfect person to write it. It will bring her back to the area while I'm here. I figured you for the matchmaking thing. Three, somehow you met Marianne Silko, and I wouldn't be at all surprised to learn that you put her up to writing those anonymous notes to Bianca. Because while Bianca is researching Jeremiah's secrets, she might as well find Brian Silko. She gets a possible bestseller and you get more Fortune heirs."

"Ridiculous," Maggie said. "How would I have ever run into Marianne and how I could have put her together with Jeremiah or the pendant?"

Ridiculous is exactly what Bianca had been thinking when Nash had started ticking things off. But he was beginning to make sense. She turned to Maggie. "How long ago did you discover the pendant and the newspaper articles in that box in the attic?"

"Years ago?" Nash pressed. "Or was it more recently

when you concocted this plan to have Bianca write Jeremiah's story? Then the pendant led you to Marianne."

"How?" Bianca asked.

"The same way it led you to her," Nash said. "Grams sits on the board of the Denver Art Museum. She's probably shopped at Caprice and she noticed the similarity in the design just as Nicola did." He turned to his grandmother. "So you visit the shop and talk to Marianne. And she not only tells you about the tradition of jewelry making in her family but she tells you about her missing brother. She probably even shows you the journal. So you suggest that she get Bianca interested with some anonymous notes. I'm betting you even paid for Marianne's plane ticket to Chicago for Bianca's book signing and then swore her to secrecy. How close am I getting?"

Maggie strode toward him until they were standing nose to nose—but that was only because Nash was still sitting down. "You must think I have some kind of superhuman psychic powers."

"I certainly did when I was a kid. Now I know you're just wicked-smart and when you decide to do something, you do it. Usually with some flair." He grinned at her scowling face. "How close am I, Grams?"

Wide-eyed, Bianca watched Maggie Fortune's frown fade and then the tiny woman burst into laughter.

Nash rose, scooped his grandmother into his arms and twirled her around in a circle. When she was on her feet again, Maggie said, "I don't just shop at Caprice. I own it. Otherwise, it's pretty much as you guessed. I found the pendant and the newspaper articles years ago. I've always been interested in Jeremiah. He reminds me of a few of my own ancestors. When I was in the process of acquiring Caprice, I noticed the similarities between the pendant and the design in Marianne's work. I naturally talked to her and when she mentioned Brian, I remembered the incident. I thought his disappearance might be a stronger bait to tempt Bianca to come back here than the black sheep of the Fortune family."

Bianca stared at the two of them. "Marianne was in on all of this? *Did* you ask her to send the anonymous notes?"

"No. That part was her idea," Maggie said. "She'd seen an interview when you'd said that you were being flooded with ideas for your next book. That girl has potential beyond jewelry design."

Bianca sat down on a chair. "She played her part perfectly. I never guessed."

"Jeremiah's genes, I suspect," Maggie said.

"And you must have read the journal," Nash guessed.

Maggie waved a hand. "I did. But the answers I need aren't all there. I want Bianca to get them. Lawyers can check into records, but they don't have much imagination or instinct for a story."

Her expression sobered as she looked down at the photos. "But I didn't foresee that you'd run into this witness protection mess. What the hell are we going to do about that?"

As if in answer, the phone on her desk rang. "Yes? You can send the general up, Grady."

"Well." Maggie turned to Nash. "You're the expert in battle strategies. James Winslow made it pretty clear to me that he wants this whole probe into Brian Silko's disappearance halted. He wants what Bianca has found so far buried. What are we going to do about him? Come up with something."

"As much as I hate to suggest it, a temporary retreat might be our best strategy," Nash said.

His grandmother's brows rose in surprise.

Nash raised a hand. "We suspect General Winslow may have a personal stake in this."

He filled his grandmother in on what they suspected about the general's possible link to Paula Harwood's family. "We don't have a shred of proof. Gabe is looking into everything in John Winslow's background in Atlanta that may have triggered his family being put into witness protection, and Nicola's father is looking into the Harwoods' disappearance on this end."

"Nick Guthrie has the right kind of connections to pry something loose. But it'll take time." Maggie turned to Nash. "I'm not fond of the idea of General Winslow shipping you off to Afghanistan. As much as I really hate backing down, your strategy may be the right one— until we have more information."

"I disagree."

Nash and Maggie turned to stare at Bianca.

"We don't know yet what role the general may have played in all of this. We may have some leverage on that score."

"What are you thinking?" Nash asked.

She shook her head. "I've just had a feeling ever since I talked to General Winslow outside your classroom yesterday. And I don't want to retreat quite yet."

Maggie shot Nash a look. "Maybe I asked the wrong person about battle strategy."

Bianca smiled at Maggie. "I'm not sure it's a strategy. But if we show General Winslow these pictures, maybe he'll fill in some of the blanks for us right away. Or give us something that will help Gabe or Nicola's father."

Maggie glanced at Nash, and at his nod, she turned to Bianca. "Go for it."

FIVE MINUTES LATER, Maggie and Nash stood on the balcony that opened off the office. General Winslow and Bianca sat at the conference table.

The general had come in armed for battle. He'd had an envelope in his hands that Nash suspected contained his immediate transfer papers. He'd refused Maggie's offer of coffee and his message had been short and sweet. Either Nash and Bianca immediately drop any further investigation into Brian Silko's disappearance or Nash would be immediately transferred to a desk job at the Pentagon. He had the papers with him.

He'd been about to hand Nash the envelope when Bianca had said, "Before you hand those orders to Nash, I think you might be interested in what we've found out about Paula Harwood." Then she gestured toward the pictures.

The instant Winslow had glanced down at the photos, the emotions that had flooded his face had been telling—shock, relief, love. Then his expression had gone blank. But he'd placed the envelope on the table next to the pictures.

Maggie kept her eyes on the two at the table as she drew Nash with her to the balcony. Keeping her voice very low, she said, "He's not so bad at strategy himself. You'd hate a desk job at the Pentagon."

"What do you know about Paula Harwood?" Bianca asked.

Nash kept his gaze focused on her as she gestured the general into a chair. Taking the seat across from him, she pulled out her notebook and said, "Let me tell you what we know and surmise."

As usual, her report was detailed and concise. When she started telling him about Jeremiah Fortune's possible connection to the Silko family, Maggie tensed at

Nash's side. He linked his hand with hers and spoke softly. "Wait. She knows what she's doing."

When she finished, Bianca met the general's eyes. "Even if you make Nash and me back off, you won't make Mrs. Fortune and her lawyers back away. If Brian is family, she'll find him. And with G.W. Securities and the FBI helping, it's only a matter of time."

"You're putting them in danger."

Bianca folded her hands on the table. "We don't want to do that. But it's more likely to happen if we're operating half-blind. I've given you everything we have. Now it's your turn. What do you know about Paula?"

For a moment the general hesitated. Then he glanced at the pictures again. "They look happy. Eleven years ago, I didn't think she'd ever look happy again."

Bianca said nothing. And Nash admired the tactic. He used it almost daily in the classroom. Students needed time to think or time to get up the courage before they would raise their hands. After a stretch of silence during which the general picked up the photos one by one and studied them, he continued, "Paula…I mean Candace— she hated the name Paula so I never called her that— Candace is my niece."

"Your brother John's daughter?" Bianca prompted.

He looked at her then. "You know about John?"

"We know that he and his family disappeared suddenly from Atlanta a dozen years ago. And we know what I've already mentioned—Paula Harwood's family was evidently in the witness protection program and they had to be relocated about the time that Cadet Silko stole that plane."

The general sighed heavily and looked back at the pictures. "It was all my fault that they had to be relocated. Twelve years ago, my sister-in-law Susan worked for Medico Inc., a company that was engaged in insurance fraud. She agreed to testify for the government. It seemed the right thing to do. Then someone nearly succeeded in killing her. Overnight, the whole family was gone."

Nash took out his cell and spoke softly to his grandmother. "I'm going to text Susan Winslow's work information to Gabe so he can check it out."

"A few months after they disappeared, my brother called me. He's the only family I have. So we kept in touch. I even visited him in Denver. We thought we were beating the system until two weeks before Susan testified. That's when she was nearly killed again. My nephew Elliot, too. Susan was driving him home from a skiing competition and someone forced them off the road. It was a miracle they weren't both killed. The marshals couldn't take the chance that the incident was an accident so the family had to be relocated again."

"What do you know about Candace?" Bianca asked.

Nash glanced at her then. It was the same question she'd asked when the two of them had first sat down at the table—except now she was using the girl's given name.

General Winslow sighed. "She called me the minute she'd learned about the relocation plans. She wanted my help. That was the first I knew she was even seeing Brian. Candace had insisted that they keep their relationship a secret because she knew her parents wouldn't like the fact that Brian was older. She claimed she and Brian were in love, but as soon as Susan and Elliot were released from the hospital, they were all leaving Denver. She was never going to be able to see Brian again."

"You wanted to help her," Bianca said.

"I wanted to save all of their lives. I caught the next plane to Denver. I was certain it was my fault that Susan and Elliot had nearly been killed. I'd refused to keep my distance. I'd kept in contact with them, visited them, and eventually, they'd been traced through me. I thought when I talked to Candace, I could make her see reason."

He paused to look at the photos again. "But they were in love. Really in love. The kind of love that you can't reason with. Candace told me she wasn't going to give him up. I believed her."

His hands were folded on the table, his knuckles white. Bianca covered his hands with one of hers. "You were afraid that history was going to repeat itself, so you agreed to help them."

General Winslow nodded. "I did."

17

NASH HEARD HIS GRANDMOTHER'S quick intake of breath. It echoed his own. He hadn't seen this coming.

"You came up with the plan for Brian to steal the airplane?" Bianca asked.

"Not at first. I tried to reason with him. He had his whole future ahead of him. But he knew as well as I did that Candace would get in touch with him and put her safety as well as the safety of her whole family at risk. He loved her too much to let her do that. So he was going to run away with her. All I had to do was put them in contact with someone who could give them a new identity."

"But you did more than that, didn't you? You also helped them get access to the plane?"

General Winslow met her eyes. "I did. Brian was a pilot. It was in his blood. With that plane and a new identity, I figured he could start up a business, make a life for my niece. It was the least I could do for him."

"And you haven't seen him since," Bianca said.

"No." He glanced at the photos again. "He agreed to never contact me or anyone in his family again."

"His mother destroyed everything but the photos. We can't trace him through those."

She waited for a minute, studying him carefully. "But you know where he is, don't you?"

There was a beat of silence before the general said, "I haven't seen either one of them or tried to contact them since the night I watched them take off in that plane."

"I didn't ask that. You strike me as a methodical person, General. You're a man who takes responsibility seriously. You helped them be together, you gave them access to the plane, arranged for new identities. I'm betting you've kept tabs on them over the years, albeit from a distance."

When he said nothing, she continued. "You haven't seen them because when you broke the rules the last time, you nearly cost your sister-in-law and your nephew their lives. So you're doing penance."

Out on the balcony, Maggie spoke softly to Nash. "She's going to bring him around. But I'm still wondering how she knew he was involved in Brian's disappearance."

"She has excellent instincts."

"I agree. So do I, and I'm betting that the general gets to see his niece again."

"And you'll get to meet Brian's family," Nash said. "Which is what you're after. But once Marianne showed you the journal, you could have hired professionals to find out what we've discovered so far."

She shot him a sideways glance. "Maybe, maybe not. The so-called professionals didn't do much to uncover the truth about that family Bianca wrote about in *Cover Up*. They sent the wrong person to jail and let a vicious killer walk around free for a long time. Besides, I want Jeremiah's and Brian's stories told. They've both suffered under a cloud. I want it lifted. To me they're both heroes."

He could agree with that. "If your lawyers can trace the genealogy to your satisfaction, how will I be related to Brian Silko exactly?"

"Something along the lines of a cousin four or five times removed." Maggie waved a hand. "I'll let the lawyers figure it out. And I don't see any reason why Marianne and her brother can't be reunited. They're not part of the witness protection program. But the rest of the family…"

"Let me guess. You want to reunite everyone."

"Twelve years is a long time. Things change. Depending on what Nick Guthrie and your friend Gabe Wilder discover, there might be a way."

She could be right. Nash glanced at Bianca. She and the general had their heads close as they talked. She wasn't taking notes, but he knew that she was recording everything in that sharp mind of hers.

"But I want an even happier ending than bringing that family together again. I want you and Bianca to have that chance that I took away from you when I coerced her into signing that contract eleven years ago. On my birthday, I even made a trip to St. Francis Church and said a prayer. But I'm backing off now. The rest is up to the two of you."

"I'm working on it, but I promised not to rush her. I did the last time, and I think that was a mistake. This time I'm letting her take the lead."

Maggie turned to study him. "Well, you must really be in love with her."

"She's it for me."

"Damn it. I knew it. Not when I meddled. Or maybe

I wouldn't have. I'd ask you if you wanted some advice, but I'm going to give it to you anyway."

She tapped a finger on his chest, then smiled at him. "You're still wearing that medal of St. Francis that I gave you for graduation from the Air Force Academy?"

"Never take it off."

"Good. Here's the advice. Patience has never been your long suit. And if your strategy worked the last time, why have you lost faith in it now? You swept the girl off her feet and got her to agree to elope with you. Think about it. I'm betting that's exactly the way Jeremiah got Falling Star away from his brother. And I always thought you took after Jeremiah."

When she moved forward into the room and joined Bianca and General Winslow at the table, Nash stayed right where he was. She'd given him an idea, and he wasn't going to wait long to try it out.

IT WAS AT LEAST AN HOUR and a half until General Winslow left, taking his envelope with him. Nash stood in the doorway with Bianca and his grandmother as they watched his car disappear down the front drive.

They'd reached a temporary stalemate. Until he was sure that his niece and Brian would be safe, General Winslow wasn't going to give up their location. But Bianca had persuaded him that they needed to find out more about just what had gone down at the Medico Inc. since that was where the problems had all started for his brother. And he'd also agreed that it wouldn't hurt if FBI special agent Nick Guthrie could find out exactly what the status of his brother's family was now.

"Good job," Maggie said as the general's car disappeared.

"It's going to take a while to get all that information,"

Bianca said. "And even then, we may all have to walk away."

"I already texted Gabe about Medico Inc. So that's one angle we're working on," Nash said. "And Nicola's father is looking at another. In the meantime, Brian and his family aren't going anywhere."

"True," Bianca said.

"But we are," Nash said, grabbing her hand.

Bianca glanced back over her shoulder at Maggie who beamed at them from the doorway. "Have fun, you two."

"Where are we going?" Bianca asked as they drove through the gates.

"I want to surprise you. Tell me what you're thinking about the stories," Nash said as he drove through the gates.

"I'm thinking that now the real work begins," she said. "In spite of the fact that we know why Brian disappeared, we're still at the beginning of the story." She leaned her head back against the seat. "The same is true of Jeremiah. There are so many questions to be answered."

He glanced at her as he turned into late afternoon Denver traffic. "All the questions—do they ever discourage you?"

"No." She smiled. "It's what attracts me to what I do. I love solving mysteries and finding the answers. And then comes the work of telling the story. That takes time, too."

"Sounds like you'll be in Denver for quite a while."

"So will you, now that the general has decided not to transfer you to the Pentagon." She glanced out the window and noticed that they were headed into the downtown area. So he wasn't taking her back to his apartment. Or to her hotel, she thought as they passed it. "I just hope it all ends happily."

"So do I."

When Nash pulled to the curb, she looked at the buildings, a string of trendy townhouses that stretched the full length of the block. "Where are...?" But her sentence trailed off when she saw the street sign on the corner. She swallowed hard as Nash opened her door and offered his hand.

"This is where the St. Francis Center for Boys used to be," she said.

"Replaced by an urban renewal project. Gabe and Jonah and I opened a new one for boys and girls near Gabe's office. Father Mike still works for us part-time."

He drew her towards one of the stoops and onto the steps so that they were out of the flow of traffic. "If my memory serves me, we're standing in front of where the garden used to be. The basketball court was just behind it. Do you remember the last time you were here?"

There was a tightness in her throat as she spoke. "Of course I do. It was the night we planned to run away to Las Vegas and get married. I came early and left you the note."

"I brought you here today to give you my reply." He took a folded piece of paper out of his pocket and offered it to her.

"Your reply?" She raised her eyes to his and saw the reckless gleam that had always pulled at her.

"I know it's a little late. But I read every word of the note you left me that night. It's only fair that you read mine."

He was right. It was only fair. Her hand only trembled slightly as she opened it.

Bianca,
I still want to marry you. Run away with me
to Vegas?"

Her heart took another tumble as her eyes flew back to his. "You can't be serious."

He put his hands on her shoulders and ran them down her arms. "I was serious the first time I asked you, but I've never been more serious than I am right now. What do you say?"

"But—"

Impatience flared in his eyes. "I know I said I'd give you time. I have."

"Three days?"

"It seems like a lifetime. And waiting around is not my style. I want to do what we never had the courage to do last time."

He had her hands now, but she didn't even try to pull away. Instead she held on.

"Something that the general said really struck home to me," Nash continued. "He said he could see his niece and Brian were really in love—the kind of love that you can't reason with. Last time we both listened to reason."

"Yes, we did."

"Maybe that was the right way for us. But I don't want to be reasonable anymore. I love you, Bianca. I did when I was nineteen, and I'm still in love with you now. Let's not be reasonable this time. Instead of letting history repeat itself, let's change it. I want a life with you—the one we've been waiting eleven years to have. So will you run away with me to Las Vegas?"

Bianca wondered how she could want to laugh and cry at the same time. She looked into his eyes and saw what she'd seen at seventeen and what she would always see—everything. "I love you, too. Much more unreasonably than I did when I was seventeen. So—" she drew in a deep breath and let it out "—this time we're going to Vegas."

"Really?" He grabbed her and pulled her far enough onto the sidewalk that he could swing her around. "You're sure?"

"I've never been more sure of anything. What will we tell your grandmother?"

"We won't," he said as he opened the car door. "At least not right away. She's sure she engineered all of this by herself."

Her brows shot up as he climbed behind the wheel. "She didn't?"

"I'm the one who said the prayer to St. Francis first," he said. "I'd forgotten all about it until she told me she'd said a prayer to the statue on her birthday. But the night that I found your note, Father Mike sat with me in the garden and told me to say a prayer. I prayed that you'd come back."

She grinned at him as he pulled away from the curb. "It took me a while."

"Thank goodness our reasonable days are over. Vegas, here we come."

Epilogue

Five Months Later
December 2

"Your grandmother knows how to throw a party." Bianca took a glass of champagne from Nash as she swept her gaze over the ballroom of the Fortune Mansion. Wreaths hung in swags along the walls, the Christmas tree nearly reached the fifteen-foot ceiling, and lights twinkled everywhere.

"No argument about that," Nash said. "But this is a special one—an early Christmas celebration with a very limited guest list."

Indeed it was. And it was a far cry from the crowd of celebrities and socialites who'd filled the terrace and gardens for Maggie's birthday party. The menu was different, too. The long buffet table offered pizzas, sliders and French fries as well as more elegant finger foods. And there was no string quartet. The people who'd gathered for a pre-Christmas celebration consisted of two families, the Winslows and the Silkos, and the short list of people who'd helped to unite them.

"Your General Winslow looks happy for the first time since I met him," Bianca said. He was standing next to a man who looked enough like him to be a twin. Susan Winslow, her arms around both Elliot and Candace, was laughing at something that Marianne Silko was saying.

At the far end of the room, the three younger Silkos had taken off their shoes and were sliding on the shiny parquet floors while Justin Bieber's latest album pumped out of the sound system.

"He *should* be happy," Nash said. "Nick Guthrie is a thorough man, and he says that the person the FBI suspected of hiring someone to kill his sister-in-law twice died in prison five years ago. And Gabe learned that Medico Inc. was liquidated as soon as her testimony put the guy in jail, so the guy lost any source of revenue he might have had to pay for revenge."

"That's what Brian is grilling Gabe about right now," Jonah said as he joined them. "After the scare those families have had, no one is quite ready to believe it might be over."

"Maggie's being cautious, too," Nash said. "You can bet that she's getting every detail she can from Nick Guthrie about what he was able to discover."

Bianca shifted her gaze to the buffet table where Maggie was deep in conversation with Nicola's father and a woman she hadn't yet met.

"Who's the leggy brunette?" Jonah asked. "She's the only one I haven't been able to place."

"She works for the new security office Gabe is open-ing in San Francisco," Nash said. "Maggie hired her to provide personal security for the Winslows until they return to the East Coast. I'm surprised you haven't run into her."

"I'll have to remedy that."

"The Winslows are seriously considering the new jobs Maggie has offered them that will allow them to move from the East Coast to the San Francisco area where Brian runs his business," Bianca said. "And they've decided that they'll all keep their current names."

"Safer. Are you ever going to be able to write your book?" Jonah asked.

"Eventually. But I have a lot of research to do still. This is the first time I've met Brian and his wife. And Brian has stories that his grandmother handed down to him about his great-great-grandfather who might very well be Jeremiah's son."

Nash took her arm, deftly moving her out of the path of an oncoming dog as it made a beeline for the children. Detective Loomis had arrived along with Sergeant MacAuliffe.

"This is a first even for Grams. She never allows animals in the ballroom."

"Or in the dining room, either," Maggie said as she joined them. "But I made an exception. I thought the children might like to meet Detective Loomis's dog." They all glanced over to see the smallest Silko climb on the animal's back. Then she sighed. "It's been a long time since anyone used these parquet floors to slide on."

"I'm tempted to join them," Nash murmured in Bianca's ear. "What do you think?"

"Nah. You're probably very skilled at it. You'd win and spoil their competition."

Maggie touched her glass to Bianca's. "Nice comeback."

"She's good," Jonah said. "She can beat him at poker, too. I think it's time he married the girl." Then he sauntered off in the direction of the brunette.

"I totally agree," Maggie said without missing a beat. And as if on her signal, Father Mike entered the room.

Nash shot Bianca a look. For five months they'd managed to keep their elopement a secret. She'd moved into his apartment as soon as they'd returned from Vegas, but neither of them had told anyone that they'd gotten married.

Nash turned to his grandmother. "Grams—"

She waved a hand to silence him. "I know all about the elopement. But it's been five months, and you haven't even given the girl a ring. And every woman wants to plan a wedding—a church wedding. You can talk to Father Mike about the arrangements after the party. I'm thinking she'd make a lovely June bride."

She patted Nash's shoulder, winked at Bianca and then walked away to greet Father Mike.

Nash took Bianca's hands in his. "We don't have to do everything she wants, you know."

She smiled at him. "I know." Then she tilted her head to study him. "Do you want to get married in a church?"

"I do as long as I'm marrying you." He reached into his pocket and brought out a small box. "I was going to wait until Christmas to ask you. The ring was my mother's. I had it sized for you."

Bianca stared at the sapphire circled in diamonds and her heart took still another tumble. "It's lovely."

"Do you want a church wedding, Bianca?"

She met his eyes. "I do as long as I'm marrying you.

This time around, we'll have both the unreasonable and the reasonable."

Across the room, Maggie linked her arm with Father Mike's and sighed as Nash slipped the ring on Bianca's finger. "Timing is everything."

* * * * *

Be sure to watch for Jonah's story in
SEXY SILENT NIGHTS,
from Harlequin Blaze.

COMING NEXT MONTH

Blaze's 10th Anniversary
Special Collectors' Editions

Available July 26, 2011

#627 THE BRADDOCK BOYS: TRAVIS
Love at First Bite
Kimberly Raye

#628 HOTSHOT
Uniformly Hot!
Jo Leigh

#629 UNDENIABLE PLEASURES
The Pleasure Seekers
Tori Carrington

#630 COWBOYS LIKE US
Sons of Chance
Vicki Lewis Thompson

#631 TOO HOT TO TOUCH
Legendary Lovers
Julie Leto

#632 EXTRA INNINGS
Encounters
Debbi Rawlins

You can find more information on upcoming
Harlequin® titles, free excerpts and more at
www.HarlequinInsideRomance.com.

HBCNM0711

REQUEST YOUR FREE BOOKS!
2 FREE NOVELS PLUS 2 FREE GIFTS!

Harlequin® *Blaze™*

red-hot reads!

Once bitten, twice shy. That's Gabby Wade's motto—
especially when it comes to Adamson men.
And the moment she meets Jon Adamson her theory
is confirmed. But with each encounter a little something
sparks between them, making her wonder if she's been
too hasty to dismiss this one!

Enjoy this sneak peek from ONE GOOD REASON
by Sarah Mayberry, available August 2011
from Harlequin® Superromance®.

Gabby Wade's heartbeat thumped in her ears as she marched to her office. She wanted to pretend it was because of her brisk pace returning from the file room, but she wasn't that good a liar.

Her heart was beating like a tom-tom because Jon Adamson had touched her. In a very male, very possessive way. She could still feel the heat of his big hand burning through the seat of her khakis as he'd steadied her on the ladder.

It had taken every ounce of self-control to tell him to unhand her. What she'd really wanted was to grab him by his shirt and, well, explore all those urges his touch had instantly brought to life.

While she might not like him, she was wise enough to understand that it wasn't always about liking the other person. Sometimes it was about pure animal attraction.

Refusing to think about it, she turned to work. When she'd typed in the wrong figures three times, Gabby admitted she was too tired and too distracted. Time to call it a day.

As she was leaving, she spied Jon at his workbench in the shop. His head was propped on his hand as he studied blueprints. It wasn't until she got closer that she saw his eyes were shut.

He looked oddly boyish. There was something innocent and unguarded in his expression. She felt a weakening in her resistance to him.

"Jon." She put her hand on his shoulder, intending to shake him awake. Instead, it rested there like a caress.

His eyes snapped open.

"You were asleep."

"No, I was, uh, visualizing something on this design." He gestured to the blueprint in front of him then rubbed his eyes.

That gesture dealt a bigger blow to her resistance. She realized it wasn't only animal attraction pulling them together. She took a step backward as if to get away from the knowledge.

She cleared her throat. "I'm heading off now."

He gave her a smile, and she could see his exhaustion.

"Yeah, I should, too." He stood and stretched. The hem of his T-shirt rose as he arched his back and she caught a flash of hard male belly. She looked away, but it was too late. Her mind had committed the image to permanent memory.

And suddenly she knew, for good or bad, she'd never look at Jon the same way again.

*Find out what happens next in ONE GOOD REASON,
available August 2011 from Harlequin® Superromance®!*

Celebrating

Blaze™ **10** *years of*
red-hot reads

Featuring a special August author lineup of
six fan-favorite authors who have written
for Blaze™ from the beginning!

The Original Sexy Six:

Vicki Lewis Thompson
Tori Carrington
Kimberly Raye
Debbi Rawlins
Julie Leto
Jo Leigh

Pick up all six Blaze™
Special Collectors' Edition titles!
August 2011

www.Harlequin.com

HBCELEBRATE0811

USA TODAY *bestselling author*

Lynne Graham

introduces her new Epic Duet

THE VOLAKIS VOW
A marriage made of secrets...

Tally Spencer, an ordinary girl with no experience of
relationships... Sander Volakis, an impossibly rich and
handsome Greek entrepreneur. Sander is expecting to
love her and leave her, but for Tally this is love at first
sight. Little does he know that Tally is expecting his
baby...and blackmailing him to marry her!

PART ONE:
THE MARRIAGE BETRAYAL
Available August 2011

PART TWO:
BRIDE FOR REAL
Available September 2011

Available only from Harlequin Presents®.

INTRIGUE

SPECIAL EDITION

Life, Love, Family and Top Authors!

IN AUGUST, HARLEQUIN SPECIAL EDITION FEATURES
USA TODAY BESTSELLING AUTHORS
MARIE FERRARELLA AND *ALLISON LEIGH.*

THE BABY WORE A BADGE
BY *MARIE FERRARELLA*

The second title in the **Montana Mavericks:
The Texans Are Coming!** miniseries....

Suddenly single father Jake Castro has his hands full with
the baby he never expected—and with a beautiful young
woman too wise for her years.

COURTNEY'S BABY PLAN
BY *ALLISON LEIGH*

The third title in the **Return to the Double C** miniseries....

Tired of waiting for Mr. Right, nurse Courtney Clay takes
matters into her own hands to create the family she's
always wanted— but her surly patient may just be
the Mr. Right she's been searching for all along.

**Look for these titles and others in August 2011
from Harlequin Special Edition wherever books are sold.**

BIG SKY BRIDE, BE MINE! *(Northridge Nuptials)* by *VICTORIA PADE*
THE MOMMY MIRACLE by *LILIAN DARCY*
THE MOGUL'S MAYBE MARRIAGE by *MINDY KLASKY*
LIAM'S PERFECT WOMAN by *BETH KERY*

SEUSA0811